A FAIRY PROMISE

ALSO BY C. J. BRIGHTLEY

Erdemen Honor:
The King's Sword
A Cold Wind
Honor's Heir

A Long-Forgotten Song:
Things Unseen
The Dragon's Tongue
The Beginning of Wisdom

Fairy King
A Fairy King

A FAIRY PROMISE

C. J. BRIGHTLEY

Egia, LLC

ISBN 978-1517371173

Published in the United Sates of America by Egia, LLC.

www.cjbrightley.com

For my parents

ONE

Silver-gold light woke Hannah, gilding her eye-lashes. She wasn't sure whether the bedroom had existed before her visit or whether Cadeyrn had conjured it for her. Her door was just beside the door to Cadeyrn's own suite, dark polished wood with a heavy handle of what appeared to be ivory. The room itself was large, though not cavernous. One entire wall was taken up with wide, arched windows looking upon a land-scape of jagged mountains behind rolling green hills, the foreground filled with a jumble of thatched roof houses. Her bed stood at the opposite wall, canopied with gauzy white silk. The floor was covered with layered rugs, the green-upon-green patterns competing in subtle harmony. Another wall had an expansive fireplace, fronted by sev-eral leather couches and velvet chairs far more expen-sive-looking than any Hannah had ever seen.

She stood and stretched, the white silk of her gown fluttering soft as butterfly wings around her legs. The room was somehow both exotic and comforting; the feel of Cadeyrn's careful, thoughtful courtesy was in every line of the furniture, every drape of fabric. A dark wooden wardrobe stood to one side, and she opened it to find her own clothes neatly folded and cleaned. *Magic*, she thought with a smile. More clothes hung on padded hangers: a fairy tale gown of deep blue velvet and silk, several dresses that were slightly less ornate, though no less beautiful, some silk blouses and shirts in white, cream, and deep jewel tones, some trousers of a thick fabric she thought might be for riding, and others. Leather boots and pearled slippers sat along the bottom.

Did Cadeyrn want her to wear these clothes? Hannah let her fingers run down the velvet of a violet gown, cut in at the waist then flaring softly outward. She pulled out the dress and held it up, finding a mirror on the inside of the wardrobe door.

The color made the alabaster of her skin nearly glow, the dark brown of her hair shining against the soft fabric. *I look like a princess.* She blinked and put the dress away. It wouldn't be right to wear the dress; it wasn't hers, even if it fit. She dressed in her own clothes and brushed her hair with an ivory-handled brush she found in a drawer inside the wardrobe.

She opened her door to peer out into the hall. The hall was floored in dove-gray stone, slightly worn in the center as if feet had trod the stone for hundreds of years. Cadeyrn's room was just next to hers, his door forming the end of the hallway. The other end disappeared down a stairwell.

Silence reigned.

She hesitated, then put her ear to Cadeyrn's door. Was he awake? Was he well, after what had happened the day before?

After she had finished the gingerbread house, he had showed her to her room and bid her good evening. He'd bent to brush his lips against her knuckles, his lips almost feverishly hot.

Hannah had lain awake for hours, but when she finally slept, it had been without dreams.

She heard nothing from Cadeyrn's room, so she knocked quietly.

Silence, then a muffled thump. She frowned, trying to interpret the sound.

Hannah had her hand raised to knock again when the door opened.

"Good morning." Cadeyrn smiled. "Did you rest well?"

"Yes, thank you."

He wore a new shirt of deep blue, crisp and immaculate, tucked into those slim breeches. The color made his eyes glitter like sapphires against his pearl-white skin. His boots were the same ones he had worn previously. His hair was wilder than she had seen it before, and she wondered whether it was styled that way on purpose, or whether it was simply disheveled from sleep.

"Would you dine with me?" He opened the door wider and gestured toward a small table by the window.

"Of course."

He held her chair out for her and then sat across from her. "What would you like to eat?" he asked, that faint accent almost imperceptibly stronger.

"Whatever you prefer. I'm not picky," Hannah replied.

Cadeyrn's lips rose in a subtle, wry smile, and he seemed to consider a moment before nodding. Plates appeared in front of them, holding small servings of gnocchi drizzled with pesto atop an artistic arrangement of mushrooms, petite squares of cheese covered in caramelized onions and peppers nestled beside exotic greens, salmon filets crusted with walnuts and brown sugar, and several more exquisitely prepared dishes.

Hannah's eyes widened. "This looks fancy."

"I thought you might be hungry, since I forgot to feed you a real meal last night. I hope you'll forgive me for that." His eyes were unexpectedly solemn, as if he actually doubted that Hannah would nod.

"Of course."

As before, he waited for her to begin before he took a bite.

"This is delicious!" Hannah said.

"Good." Cadeyrn smiled, his eyes sparkling.

They ate in silence for several minutes. Hannah wondered what to say, then wondered whether he was uncomfortable in the silence or whether he thought it was peaceful. She glanced up to see Cadeyrn put his fork down a little clumsily. He took a deep breath through his nose, his gloved hand clenching the side of the table.

"What's wrong?"

Cadeyrn was breathing too quickly, his eyes halfclosed. "A passing dizziness. That's all." He turned his chair to the side and rested his elbows on his knees, letting his head hang down. His shirt stretched tight across his shoulders, outlining lean, hard muscles.

Without thought, Hannah knelt on the floor beside him. His breaths were ragged, a little catch in each inhalation. His right hand clenched and relaxed, then clenched again, as if he'd forgotten to pretend that he was fine.

"Are you in pain?" she whispered.

"Not exactly," he gasped.

Hannah bit her lip as she watched him breathe, studying the still-dark shadows beneath his eyes, the tightness of his thin lips.

After some moments, the struggle seemed to fade, and his tense shoulders relaxed a little. He seemed to sag in his chair. He muttered something unintelligible.

"What was that?" Hannah asked, her voice as gentle as she could make it.

Cadeyrn drew back into himself, a little breathless but fully composed. "I beg your pardon." He straightened, pulling his dignity around him like a cloak.

Hannah straightened as well, though she remained kneeling. "What's wrong, Cadeyrn? Please tell me."

"Repercussions." He raised one eyebrow at her, his expression somehow both mocking and kind. "Consequences. Not entirely expected, but in retrospect I should have known."

"It's because of me?" Unexpected tears filled her eyes.

Faster than thought, he had pulled her to her feet, and stood in front of her, his eyes blazing. "It is because of what *I* did. I had a choice, and I made it willingly, for honor and love and hope. I don't regret it, and neither should you." He stopped, his gaze holding hers. His nostrils flared slightly as he inhaled and exhaled, keeping the rhythm steady with iron control.

Hannah was caught by his magnificent beauty, the brilliance of his eyes, and the intensity of his voice.

Then he turned his head, his attention caught by a tiny sound at the door. He flicked a finger and the door opened.

A tiny yellow bird flew across the room and landed on Cadeyrn's gracefully outstretched hand. It chattered at him.

"Tell him, with all due respect, that I will be down momentarily."

The bird shot across the room and disappeared down the hallway.

Cadeyrn's blue eyes focused on Hannah. "Your pardon. I have a distinguished guest I must receive."

Hannah glanced at the table. "I'm full enough. Should I come with you, or do you want me to wait here?" She frowned a little worriedly, studying his face.

The cool winter light caught the dull purple-grey undertone of his skin, his pallor highlighted by the deep navy of his shirt. He blinked, as if surprised by the thought. "Would you wish to come?"

"I don't want to intrude."

He tilted his head, his gaze sharp on her face, then the corners of his mouth quirked upward. "I would be honored if you would accompany me." He offered her his arm.

She slipped her hand into the crook of his elbow, feeling her face heat. Her fingers rested lightly on the hollow at the bottom of his bicep, fine cords of tendons beneath his skin. *He's so thin and hard. I wonder what his life is really like. There is so much I cannot imagine, and so much he hasn't said.*

Cadeyrn strode toward the door, leading her down a long hallway with a bare stone floor, then down a wide, curving staircase. On the last step he stumbled, then put out a hand against the wall. He stopped, his gloved fingers flat against the stone.

"Are you all right?"

"A moment, please," he breathed.

14

Hannah hesitated, then, wondering at her own courage, slipped an arm around his waist. The smooth, pale skin of his throat moved as he swallowed, and she blushed as she felt the warmth of his skin beneath the fabric of his shirt.

He straightened, and she shifted away, letting her arm fall.

Cadeyrn continued a short way, stopping before a heavy wooden door. He closed his eyes and raised his chin, controlled his breathing, then opened the door and strode in.

Hannah followed, feeling the power swirling in his wake. The door had opened into a large room, the floor and walls of white marble, the ceiling vaulted far overhead. Long, thin tapestries lined the walls, the detail far too intricate to be deciphered from dozens of feet away. The room reminded Hannah of a small cathedral, or a large chapel, though none of the tapestries or imagery was especially religious. Perhaps it was only the finely wrought marble columns, or the magnificent ribs of the vaulted ceiling. At the end of the room to Hannah's left was a low dias on which sat a throne. This throne, unlike the one in the lower throne room she had seen before, was made of white marble and covered in intricate gold and silver inlay, broad whorls surrounding smaller flowers and leaves.

Cadeyrn stood some distance in front of the throne facing Comonoc, the centaur king.

Cadeyrn's drawings had been accurate in every detail save one; Hannah had not realized how very *big* Comonoc was. The drawings had shown that his equine body was heavily proportioned, more like a draft horse than a thoroughbred. But she had not understood from the pictures that his withers were easily seven feet above the ground, and his human shoulders were just as broad, perhaps broader, than his equine body. His massive biceps were each larger than her waist. The bow slung across his heavily-muscled shoulders must have been seven feet long.

Comonoc bowed deeply, his human body and equine legs more graceful than Hannah would have imagined possible. His voice rumbled. Hannah didn't understand his words, but she understood the respect in them.

Cadeyrn answered him, then said, "Let us converse in English, if you please. I have a guest." He motioned toward Hannah.

The centaur turned toward her, and Hannah took an involuntary step backward. He tilted his head, studying her, then turned back to Cadeyrn.

"Your Majesty," Comonoc said, "Am I to understand that this human child is the cause of your... precipitous action last even?"

Cadeyrn's lips rose in a thin smile. "Do you think I am so easily unseated? Do not fear. I am already recovering."

Comonoc took a step closer, looming far above Cadeyrn's slight form. He leaned forward slightly, as if he meant to have a staring contest with the Fae monarch. A tense moment passed. Then Cadeyrn swayed; he would have fallen but Comonoc's great hands caught him around the shoulders.

Comonoc held him on his feet, the centaur's lips curled in anger and worry. Hannah's heart constricted at the sight Cadeyrn's pale face, his eyelids closed, flopped over Comonoc's wrist. "What can I do?" she whispered.

The centaur king rumbled, "I think you've done quite enough. His strength is a thousand times that of mine; normally that slight nudge I gave him would no more have swayed him than you could blow over a mountain."

Cadeyrn blinked and straightened, shrugging his shoulders out of Comonoc's grasp with firm courtesy. "You've made your point, Comonoc." He was a little breathless, and despite his insistence at standing on his own, he seemed to waver again.

"Your pardon, Your Majesty." Comonoc bowed again. "I would not have been so discourteous if I were not so concerned. My people felt the concussion of your deed across our lands."

Cadeyrn's eyes widened. "You felt it even there?"

Comonoc grunted; the stone beneath Hannah's feet trembled. "No one but you, Your Majesty, would have attempted such a feat, and if they did, they would not have lived to lament their failure."

Cadeyrn closed his eyes and swallowed, as if forcing back dizziness.

Comonoc sighed heavily. "Sit, Your Majesty. I do not wish to see you fall."

"I'm fine," Cadeyrn murmured. He looked anything but fine, his lips a bloodless white.

The centaur king drew back, his nostrils flaring, though Hannah wasn't sure if he was angry or merely worried. "I came not only to give you my respect and honor, and to assure myself that you were yet alive, but also to stand by you. For behind me rides Einion."

If Hannah had not been looking so closely, she would have missed the bleak expression that flickered over Cadeyrn's face, instantly replaced by a resigned sort of wry acceptance.

"He felt it too, did he?" Cadeyrn's lips pressed together. "I had not expected that, but I did make the decision in haste." He glanced up at Comonoc and smiled thinly. "And before you ask, I don't regret it. I have had succession plans in place for many years."

Comonoc blinked. "No one is ready. Madoc is but a child, and Maeve even younger. Colwyn... with respect, I wouldn't recommend him, Your Majesty. Besides, I came to fight for you. It is a legal issue, not a war. He wants a duel, as is his right. I request the honor of serving as your second."

Cadeyrn's smile deepened in genuine amusement, his eyes sparkling. "I would have no other. Who better but you? You've known grief and triumph. You'd understand the responsibility."

The centaur froze, then his eyes widened. "You have designated me?" His deep voice cracked. "That is unwise, my lord. I am not suited to be high king!"

"Thus you prove the wisdom of my choice." Cadeyrn glanced at Hannah. "There is one thing yet to do. Hannah must be returned to her home before Einion arrives. Cara can take her, if you open the way for him. I have not the strength to do it alone now. Not yet. In another day, perhaps, but I doubt we have that much time."

Comonoc's frown deepened. "I cannot do it alone, Your Majesty. No one but you..."

Cadeyrn raised a hand and the white owl swooped down to him from somewhere above. He brought the owl closer to his face and murmured softly to the bird. Cara hooted and shuffled his wings.

Hannah imagined that the owl looked worried, his great orange eyes glowing as he turned his head and stared at her. The centaur's expression was more clear; he scowled at Cadeyrn, the great muscles of his arms bunched and tense.

"I beg you reconsider, Your Majesty," he rumbled. "Let me fight for you!"

Cadeyrn waved his free hand and produced a small table. Atop the table was a shallow silver bowl filled with water, a goblet, and a small, sharp knife with a jeweled hilt. "Your objections have been noted." He lowered his hand, waiting while Cara sidled up to perch on his shoulder. Then he leaned forward, resting both hands on the table as he stared into the water. "Einion is close. We don't have much time." He looked up. "Hannah, come here please."

Her mouth dry, Hannah stepped closer. Cadeyrn's face was tight and pale, his eyebrows drawn slightly downward in an unconscious frown.

"What are you going to do?" she whispered.

He licked his lips and took a deep breath, meeting her eyes with his brilliant blue gaze. "Comonoc does not have the depth of magic that I do, so he cannot make a way for you alone. Neither does Cara have the strength; he is old, and carrying a person between worlds is a much greater task than carrying letters that I have imbued with magic to ease his way. I will lend them both some of my strength, and between them they will return you to your home.

"Cara…" Cadeyrn closed his eyes and sighed softly. "I doubt Cara will be able to make the return journey. I ask your hospitality for him for the rest of his life. He understands English, Welsh, and French. It grieves me to bid farewell to such a faithful friend, but perhaps it is for the best." He turned to look at the owl on his shoulder, who stared back for a moment before pressing its face against Cadeyrn's cheek.

His gloved fingers were steady as he rolled up his left sleeve. Hannah watched with wide eyes, wondering what he intended to do.

Cadeyrn took up the knife and slashed his forearm.

"What are you doing?" Hannah cried.

19

Cadeyrn's voice was a little tight as he murmured, "Blood is strength, you know. In legend and myth and religion and human medicine, blood is significant." The blood ran in a thin silver stream from his arm into the goblet.

Cadeyrn dipped the gloved fingertips of his right hand into the goblet and lifted his hand, dripping silver blood over Cara's feathered head. Again he did it, dragging the silver blood down Cara's white back and wings. A third time, smearing around the owl's eyes and down his chest, over his thin legs and sharp talons. Then Cadeyrn lifted the goblet, and Cara dipped his beak into it. Hannah didn't see whether the white owl actually drank any of the blood, but the thought of it made her dizzy.

She was breathing too fast, her vision going fuzzy around the edges. "Don't do this," she whispered.

Comonoc bent his head, eyes closed, and Cadeyrn smeared quicksilver blood over his forehead, down his nose, over his cheeks, and on his chin. Then he handed the centaur the goblet, and Comonoc, frowning in dismay, drained it.

Silver blood dripped over Cadeyrn's left glove to dot the floor. "Is it enough?" he murmured, watching Comonoc with steady eyes.

The centaur hesitated, then nodded. "Yes, Your Majesty."

Cadeyrn smoothed his right hand over the wound and the bleeding stopped. He leaned both gloved hands on the table and peered into the bowl of water, then looked up at Hannah.

"Do not be afraid, dearest Hannah. This will keep you safe."

"What about you?" Her heartbeat thundered in her ears.

He smiled, a sudden flash of reckless beauty. "Oh, Hannah, you've given me more joy in the past week than I've felt in years. Einion has been waiting for an excuse to demand a duel since the end of the war. Even the high king is subject to the laws of Faerie, and I broke a very old law when I broke the hold of the goblin fruit on you. I didn't expect him to feel it so far away, but his claim to a duel is just and I will answer it. If you don't go home now, you may be trapped forever. Einion would delight in your captivity, and none of my kin are near enough, or strong enough, to take you home. Now is your chance." He stepped forward and faced her, his eyes glittering.

Are those tears in his eyes?

"Dearest Hannah, I thank you for your friendship. Fare thee well, now and always." He bent to kiss her hand, his lips trembling and far too hot against her skin.

As he straightened, he wavered a little, his fingers tight on hers, then slipping away. "Cara." He turned, letting the owl press its face against his cheek again. "Fare thee well, old friend." Then he looked up at the centaur looming over his shoulder. "Now, Comonoc."

Cadeyrn's eyes flicked back to hers, brilliant azure glinting in the light that seemed to burst upon her vision. Comonoc roared something Hannah didn't understand, then everything seemed to splinter apart, light and shadow tumbling together, entwined reflections of stone arches, tree branches, starlight.

Cara's talons gripped Hannah's shoulders as if he had become enormous, his wings beating above her in frantic rhythm. He screamed, the sound entirely unlike anything an owl might make.

"No! I don't want to leave him!" Hannah cried, writhing in Cara's grip. The talons tightened on her, cutting through the cloth into her skin. "I wish I could help him!"

21

The world skittered sideways, turned inside out and upside down. Hannah and Cara tumbled over each other across a stone floor.

Hannah sprawled on the floor, gasping and dizzy. She'd hit her head as she tumbled, and she blinked sparkles from her eyes, trying not to groan at the thudding pain. Cara hooted softly a few feet away, one wing held away from his body.

Then Hannah looked up.

Cadeyrn stood with his back to her, his feet planted solidly on the stone floor. Comonoc stood off to the side, arrow nocked and aimed at a slim figure just in front of Cadeyrn.

"So much for your chivalry. It appears she'd rather stay and watch the fun." The Fae gave a sharp-toothed grin that made Hannah's stomach turn.

"She isn't part of this, Einion. Your duel is with me." Cadeyrn shifted slightly, blocking Hannah's view of the strange Fae's face, and she breathed a sigh of desperate relief.

Einion had a narrow, fine-boned face and pale, almost pearlescent skin much like Cadeyrn's, though without the grey undertone that so worried Hannah. He'd bared those pointed teeth in a dangerous, glittering smile. He was breathing heavily.

"Oh, but she *wished*! She wished to help you, Cadeyrn. Who am I to deny such a favored one a wish?" Einion's words dripped through the air, sweet as honey.

Hannah found herself standing, Einion to her left, Cadeyrn to her right. More time must have passed for them than she had experienced. Cadeyrn looked even worse, though she hadn't imagined it was possible. The dark circles beneath his eyes had deepened, his cheeks sunken so that his eyes stood out too bright beneath long, dark lashes. His hair looked wilder than ever. Both he and Einion were holding long, narrow swords.

A breeze flicked Hannah's hair into her face, and she shook it out of her eyes. They were no longer in the throne room; a grassy expanse spread out around them in all directions. Some two hundred yards away in all directions, stone walls rose into the sky, the top edge disappearing into the brilliant blue.

"What is this place?" Hannah murmured, not expecting an answer.

Einion gestured grandly, the razor-sharp tip of his sword cutting the air mere inches from her face. "This, dear one, is the Royal Dueling Ground. This soil has drunk the blood of legends and myths, kings and challengers and beasts the like of which you have never even dreamed. Even mortal blood, though your kind are not often so honored." He dropped the tip of his sword and circled Hannah, studying her as he caught his breath.

"I propose a challenge," he said at last. "By law, and by the wish you so carelessly made, you are permitted to *help* the high king."

Hannah's mouth went even drier. "I've never used a sword before," she breathed.

Einion laughed, the sound like shattered glass. "That would be no fun! Besides, it would be *unwise* to flaunt the laws so flagrantly. Unlike Cadeyrn, I take my obligations seriously."

Cadeyrn blinked slowly, as if considering whether to dignify the insult with a response.

"I propose a challenge of virtues. Cadeyrn and Comonoc can attest that it is fair and in accordance with the Code." He smiled at Cadeyrn and licked his lips. "Three times she will choose between two options that I will devise. One will represent you and your continued reign.

The other will represent your downfall and my ascendance, with my court, to the throne of the high king."

Hannah felt her heart thudding raggedly. *But that's not helping. That's… deciding everything!* "Cadeyrn, I don't think…"

Cadeyrn turned his eyes toward her, and she stopped, caught in the intensity of his gaze. He was telling her something, if only she could understand it.

"I…"

"Hannah will not be harmed or threatened in any way by the test itself or the consequences of any of her decisions." Cadeyrn licked his lips and his tongue left a silver sheen on the pale skin. "Regardless of her choices and the outcome of the challenge, she will be returned to her home safely, when she desires, to the time at which she left. You and yours will not harm her now or later, in this world or hers."

"Agreed."

"Her choices will be judged by the assembled monarchs of the Seelie and Unseelie courts. All will be bound by the Code to judge without partiality or preference."

"Agreed." Einion smiled easily. "With full knowledge of our choices within the test, both real and imagined… yours, mine, and hers."

Cadeyrn nodded sharply. "And I will speak with Hannah, in confidence, before the challenge begins."

"For what purpose?" Einion's eyes narrowed.

"I owe you no explanation, Einion."

Einion's mouth twisted in anger, but he nodded sharply. "As you say."

Cadeyrn hesitated, glanced at Hannah again, and gave a minute nod.

"All right," Hannah breathed.

Einion strode some distance away and turned his back on them, sheathing his sword and crossing his arms. Cadeyrn waved a hand and the almost inaudible rustle of the breeze in the grass disappeared, leaving Cadeyrn and Hannah cocooned in silence.

Cadeyrn's jaw was tight as he turned his gaze toward her.

He's angry at me. The thought startled her, and she turned it over in her mind, almost missing Cadeyrn's quiet voice when he began to speak.

"Human wishes don't have power, exactly. But Fae, or fairies as you sometimes call us, are bound by rules. We can bend these rules to some degree, but there are consequences to doing so; the more we bend the rules, the harsher the consequences. These laws are outside of us; they are a fact of magic, as gravity is a fact of matter. In granting a human's wish, fairies do not actually gain *power*, but we gain the ability to do things we would not otherwise be able to do.

"But fairies don't always grant the wish exactly as the human expects. Nor does the wish, even if granted exactly as expected, always have the consequences the human desired... or at least, not *only* those consequences."

Cadeyrn stopped and swallowed, as if fighting dizziness.

"Are you all right?" Hannah breathed. "You look..."

He glanced up, his azure eyes unexpectedly cool. "The answer to your question is irrelevant. What matters is this: Unscrupulous fairies, such as Einion, the Unseelie king, would not normally grant human wishes. Certainly not out of kindness or good will. But he might, and has, because he wants to twist your wish to his own ends.

"There are rules to wish-granting that affect both the human wisher and the fairy granting the wish. Rules are both legal and conceptual. The words you say matter. If the fairy accepts the wish but fails to grant it, either through cheating or for more innocent reasons, they will suffer consequences. The human would be released from any responsibility they might have accepted as part of the wish. It is expected that a cunning fairy will use the 'fine print', so to speak, and there is no penalty for that." His eyes glittered with emotion. "Wishing in front of a fairy is a dangerous business."

Hannah's hands were trembling so badly that she shoved them in her jeans pockets. Through a tight throat, she whispered, "But you granted my wishes. Was that dangerous?"

Cadeyrn's eyes didn't leave hers. "I did. It was permitted, and I acted within the law."

"You were generous."

Cadeyrn's tightly held anger seemed to soften almost imperceptibly. "I meant to be. I will always be generous to you, Hannah. As long as I live." His eyes flicked toward Einion and then back to her.

"Einion won't be, though. I don't trust him, or this test. He'll cheat." Hannah tried, and failed, to keep her voice steady.

"I mentioned penalties for the fairy. Penalties for failing a wish or overtly breaking faith can vary, but usually the fairy is imprisoned inside an object of the wisher's choosing until he grants three additional wishes to the wisher. There is no time limit on this. The fairy remains bound to the object and cannot leave or act in any other way until either the human uses the three wishes or the object is destroyed. The fairy may not seek direct or indirect retribution after the penalty, and the ability to twist the wishes to the fairy's ends is much more tightly restricted.

"If the human dies prior to making their last wish, the penalty does not end. Whoever inherits possession of the object also inherits the wishes."

26

Hannah's eyes suddenly widened. "Like a genie!"

"Yes; fairies are the origin of that myth." Cadeyrn stopped and closed his eyes, then shook his head slightly, as if the dizziness were rising again. "A durable object is a good choice if the wisher intends to imprison the fairy for a long time. Bronze, for example." His gaze intensified. "It doesn't rust or corrode; it could be dropped in the sea and survive for millennia. A more merciful object might be wooden; when it rots, the fairy is freed. The object must be made, like a lamp or stool or spoon, rather than a mountain or a river." He stopped again, his nostrils flaring as he breathed slowly through his nose. "The point is, he will undoubtedly try to structure the test to his advantage, but he will not cheat through outright deception. To do so would cost him the challenge.

"Einion will have you choose three times, each time between two choices. In each, one of the choices represents Einion and one represents me. I have no idea how these representations will be made. You must honestly choose as you believe best. Even if you think you can guess which represents me and which represents Einion, and if you wished to choose in such a way as to help me, to choose other than how you truly believe best would be a lie, and that would forfeit *everything*."

Hannah swallowed.

"The consequences would be worse than anything you imagine. Besides, a lie would be dishonorable. You would not intentionally dishonor yourself so, and I would not willingly triumph in such a way."

Hannah nodded, her heart pounding. "I think... I hope... I'd choose the way you would rather than the way Einion would."

He nodded almost imperceptibly. "Perhaps so. However, Einion is devising the challenge; it is his right

27

and duty. He will design situations that he thinks are to his advantage. He is clever, and much older than he looks; he has long experience in subtlety and deviousness. He will attempt to construct situations in which you will favor his way of thinking. Even if you would choose as I would in ninety situations out of one hundred, Einion needs only find three—actually two— in which you favor his ideas. Two out of three will decide." He closed his eyes, and a muscle in his jaw tightened.

"You're afraid, aren't you?" She breathed. "Not for yourself, though. Are you? What will happen to you if I lose?"

Cadeyrn's mouth twisted. "That is irrelevant. My concern is for my kingdom; Einion would be an intelligent and practical monarch, both clever and cruel. I fear for Comonoc, and other friends, under his rule. Also, Einion is no friend to humans."

Fear made her breath come short.

The fairy king's eyes burned into her, and he opened his mouth as if he intended to say something else. Then he pressed his lips together and twitched a finger; the silence disappeared and the breeze caressed her cheek.

Within the blink of an eye, they were surrounded by creatures who seemed to step out of the air. They were all of different species: Comonoc the centaur king; a magnificent griffin with a sleek black head and razor talons flexed beneath her lion's body; a bundle of feathered wings with no visible head or feet that flapped and spun with bizarre grace some distance above the ground; a satyr with a lecherous grin; a graceful column of water that formed and reformed the shape of a slim, elegant woman; a group of flying creatures of various shapes, of which only some were humanoid. Hundreds of species surrounded them; Hannah caught her breath in surprise and awe.

Einion smiled at her toothily. "Let the challenge begin."

Hannah blinked, and the world changed.

TWO

Hannah sat on a throne dressed in jewel-encrusted gown of deep red silk. Before her stood a silent crowd of goblins and fairies, with a few centaurs, a griffin, an odd snake-bird creature, and a group of ink-dark shadows that crept along up the wall in one corner away from any of the other creatures. The throne felt familiar, the sense of responsibility and authority a comfortable weight upon her.

Einion stood at her left and Cadeyrn at her right, both silent. The scent of stone and gold was in the air, magic at her fingertips.

A fairy knelt before her, his eyes on the floor and face mostly hidden beneath his wild blond hair. Something about his shoulders seemed stoically resigned.

"As you can see, Your Majesty, the facts of the matter are not in dispute," Einion said, his voice clear and impartial. "His words and flagrant disregard of Your Majesty's authority and the crown bring shame and dishonor upon himself and Your Majesty. He knew this, and yet chose to so dishonor himself and the crown. This merits death."

Hannah glanced at Cadeyrn. *Have I seen these people before? I feel I should trust him more than Einion, but I don't remember why. How long have I been queen?*

She swallowed, pushing the thought away. "But he broke no laws?"

Einion nearly snarled, "No, Your Majesty."

Hannah took a deep breath, turning her decision over in her mind. *He broke no laws. But he slandered me. How much does that matter? Is it a matter of my ego or a matter of the honor of the office of the queen?*

It isn't about me. I don't care that much, and even if I did, it wouldn't be right to punish someone for hurting my feelings.

But the dignity of the throne is important.

She chewed her lip, then said, "He shall be banished, never to return. His family shall not be hindered from visiting him wherever he resides, but he shall not enter the kingdom again on pain of death."

Einion blinked. "What? That isn't one of the choices. He must be either executed or released."

"I am the queen. I am not ruling on a law, but for the good of the kingdom. My decision stands." She gave Einion a cold look. *Pretty arrogant for an advisor, I think! I need to keep an eye on him.*

She blinked, and the arrangement of people before her changed.

EVERY FACE SEEMED CLEARER and more vivid. The snake-bird creature was called a Haronis; it was dangerous and unpredictable, but loyal to the Seelie king. The shadows were more dangerous, unallied but tending to support the Unseelie. *Why are they here?* She pushed down the fear that threatened to choke her and turned toward the fairy kneeling before her.

"As you have heard, Your Majesty, the facts of the case are not in doubt. The suspect sold information to your enemy. He claims desperation; Iorwerth has his betrothed captive. He hoped, by betraying you, to save her." Einion's lips curved in a faint, disgusted smile. "Treason is punishable by death. Yet he has been a loyal subject all his life. He also has many devoted friends who may react... badly... if he is executed. For the sake of your throne, Your Majesty, I respectfully request that you carefully consider the consequences of your decision."

The unknown fairy turned his pale face up to her, blue-green eyes tormented. "I ask no mercy, Your Majesty. I deserve none. But I ask forgiveness, because I have always loved you and supported your reign."

Einion murmured, "Shall he be pardoned, Your Majesty, or executed?"

Hannah glanced at Cadeyrn. He returned her gaze, but she read nothing in his eyes, no hint or direction. His face was absolutely expressionless.

Hannah took a shuddering breath, twisting her fingers together in her lap. Her mouth felt dry as bone. She had to try twice before her words were audible. "Treason is punished by death. Though it grieves me, this case is no exception. Laws against treason are for the good of the kingdom, and I will not flout them no matter how my heart wishes I would."

Einion's eyes seemed to flash, and the world changed.

HANNAH REACHED UP, feeling her cheeks wet with tears. *Why am I weeping? I don't remember.*

A third fairy, his face unfamiliar, knelt before her.

Einion said, "As you have heard, Your Majesty, the facts of the case are undisputed. This criminal was exiled three years ago. He had committed crimes, all serious but none carrying capital punishment, and in your mercy you elected to banish him from the kingdom. Some weeks ago he requested entry to Tref Dwr, your largest port. In your name and with your approval, he was promised free entry and exit to the port provided that he truthfully report on the foreign ports he had visited. He did so. Before departing, he murdered the man who reported him to the watch for the crimes for which he was exiled. He is unquestionably guilty. His only defense is your promise that he will be allowed to depart safely."

The fairy looked up and smiled slightly, the expression both mocking and gently humorous. *He thinks he's going to get away with it.* "I trust your word, Your Majesty. Your honor is unquestionable."

Einion murmured, "He takes advantage of you, Your Majesty. He presumes too much and drags your name through the filth of his crimes." His voice remained low, but his anger nearly shook the room.

Hannah glanced at Cadeyrn, wondering what he would think. As before, his expression was carefully blank, his eyes intense but giving her no guidance.

Hannah swallowed bile. "Allowing him to play me for a fool is worse than revoking the safe passage I promised him. He shall be executed."

Cadeyrn let out a soft huff of air, as if he had been hit very hard. Einion's pointed teeth gleamed as he grinned.

The world shattered.

THREE

Hannah fell to her knees and retched as the world reassembled itself. She had no attention to spare for Einion's triumph or Cadeyrn's disconcerting silence; her head was spinning too fast.

Gasping, she straightened to see Cadeyrn facing Einion. The assembled fairy monarchs watched, the silence alive with tension.

"What happened?" she whispered.

Einion's grin widened. "You chose! Oh, how you chose. It was close, a brilliant challenge." He laughed, and the sound was like shards of pain in Hannah's heart. He bowed mockingly. "Cadeyrn, I admit I thought you a fool for choosing a human as a potential queen. But she surprised me. She was *marvelous*, Cadeyrn! Perhaps I will keep her."

"You swore she would be returned to her home," Cadeyrn growled. "Even you cannot break that oath."

"I swore she would be returned to her home *when she chose.*" Einion's smile widened, a flash of gleeful anticipation. "I can be very persuasive." He turned his bright, triumphant gaze upon Hannah. "*Power*, Hannah. As you have seen, I can be generous with my friends and allies. I offer you a position as an advisor in my court." His smile softened, affection and admiration shining in his face. "A *close* advisor."

Hannah's mouth was so dry she couldn't speak, and she looked desperately toward Cadeyrn. His nostrils flared with barely contained rage, his fingers clenching spasmodically on the hilt of his sword.

"I see you doubt the judgment. Let the jury explain." Einion gestured grandly.

Hannah turned wide eyes toward Comonoc, who was apparently speaking for the assembled monarchs.

"Your first choice was between honor and the law. His Majesty High King Cadeyrn would have released the offender without punishment because he broke no laws. His Majesty Einion would have executed the offender because he dishonored the crown. The round goes to Einion."

"But..." Hannah felt herself floundering. "But Cadeyrn..." She glanced at him. "He would have..."

Cadeyrn gave a sharp nod. "I would have released him without punishment. Your decision was for Einion."

She looked back at the other Fae. "But you would have chosen in anger! Wouldn't you?"

Einion shrugged easily. "Irrelevant. The choice was between honor and the law. Cadeyrn would have upheld the law at the expense of his own honor. I would have upheld my own honor."

The breeze caressed Hannah's neck, fluttering her hair so that it sent a shiver down her spine. "But…"

"You broke the rules." Comonoc's deep voice was implacable. "Breaking the rules was unprecedented. You did not choose for the law, as His Majesty High King Cadeyrn would have done, and you did not choose for personal honor, as His Majesty Einion would have done. You punished the accused although he broke no law. Your choice was perhaps wiser than either of the choices presented to you, so the ruling is… close… but our decision stands."

"Fine. What about the others?" she whispered.

"In the second case, your choice was between mercy and the law. The traitor was loyal to you, yet committed treason out of desperation and love of his betrothed. Your decision was to execute him, despite your sympathy and friendship. The round goes to Cadeyrn."

Hannah blinked. "It does?"

"He would have upheld the law. Don't you agree, Cadeyrn?" Einion smiled.

"Yes. The laws against treason are for the good of the kingdom. My own grief is irrelevant." His voice was nearly inaudible.

Comonoc stamped a hoof. "In contrast, His Majesty Einion would have pardoned the traitor, because to execute him would risk unrest from his friends and family. His Majesty Einion is accustomed to allies who are not entirely trustworthy, and this one is one of the less dangerous ones."

Einion smiled. "I would have put the traitor in a position where he could do little harm. Perhaps I would have brought one of his children into the palace to be educated as a guest of the crown… and a convenient pressure point in the future. Perhaps he would earn back the favor he had lost. Or, if necessary, I could arrange an accident later. But you, and His Majesty the High King, chose to execute him. Who is the merciful one between us?"

"Enough," Cadeyrn murmured. Einion's mouth snapped shut, but his eyes gleamed with barely suppressed mirth.

Comonoc said, "As we judged, the round goes to Cadeyrn. And the third…"

Einion grinned. "The third was magnificent! Your choice was between honoring your word and letting a crime go unpunished. Cadeyrn would have released him, honoring his word above all. I would have executed him. Your decision was like mine, and the round goes to me." His sharp-toothed grin widened.

"But…" Hannah sucked in a breath. "You would have been angry! You would have chosen to punish him in anger. I didn't! I ruled for the honor of the office of the queen. That's what Cadeyrn would have done, even if we went about it different ways."

Einion and Cadeyrn looked at each other, as if weighing something Hannah couldn't perceive.

Comonoc sighed. "His Majesty Einion is right. It is true that His Majesty High King Cadeyrn would have released the prisoner to honor his promise, and it is also true that His Majesty Einion would have broken his word to execute the offender for his undisputed crime. It is true that your choice is like that of His Majesty Einion's in result but His Majesty High King Cadeyrn's in motivation. The jury has weighed these factors, and the round goes to His Majesty Einion. Thus the challenge goes to His Majesty Einion, King of the Unseelie."

Einion's laughter rang out.

"He cheated me!" Hannah cried.

Einion froze, his eyes glinting dangerously. "In what way did I cheat you?"

"You didn't grant my wish!" Blood thundered in her ears, terror and outrage warring with each other. Out of the corner of her eye, she saw Comonoc shift uneasily.

The Unseelie Fae smiled. "I most certainly did! You not only participated in the decision, you were the deciding factor." He bowed mockingly.

"And how, exactly, did this help him? My wish was that I could help him. And yet I failed, didn't I?"

Einion's smile flickered, then returned. "You had a chance. It was even fairer than I had anticipated. The contest was closer than I had intended."

"Did you grant my wish that I help him? I don't think I wished for a *chance* to help. I said I wanted to actually help. I think that's what you agreed to…"

Einion snarled something unintelligible, then stood still, his hands by his sides.

The centaur's eyes widened and a slow, awed smile broke over his face. "Is that true?"

Hannah glanced at Cadeyrn to find him staring at her, azure eyes far too bright in his pale face.

"Choose his prison," he murmured.

Hannah couldn't find her breath for a moment. "I… um…" She couldn't look away from Cadeyrn. His terrible beauty seemed drawn thin. He was trembling. "A… a… lamp. A bronze lamp."

Cadeyrn gestured, and a lamp appeared. Einion flickered, the world shifted and spun, and Einion was gone.

Cadeyrn whispered, "Close your eyes."

WHEN SHE OPENED THEM again, they stood in Cadeyrn's sitting room. A bronze lamp sat on the table between them; light glinted on etched whorls in the surface.

Cadeyrn turned away and stumbled to the window. Both gloved hands on the windowsill, he stared across the rolling green hills as if he had never seen them before.

Finally, he murmured, "You made me a liar."

The pain in his voice took Hannah's breath away. "How?"

"I swore you would be safe." He turned and leaned against the wall, folding his arms over his chest as if he wanted to keep her words out. *Press his pain inward.* "I was prepared to sacrifice my life and my kingdom to keep that vow, and you wished it away as if it were nothing. What you did was the very antithesis of safe!" His voice shook, a cold anger underlying his controlled tone.

"Safety is overrated," she whispered. She felt herself trembling. *Why does he not understand? How can he be so angry, so hurt, when all I wanted was to help?*

The air seemed to still, and Cadeyrn said softly, "Explain." He didn't add *please*, and the discourtesy jarred her. Was it anger or merely confusion that made him terse?

"I was afraid for you! How would you feel if someone forced you to take the safe way out, even if you valued something else more than safety?" She found herself brushing away indignant tears. "I'm not a child, Cadeyrn. I appreciate your protection, but I have the right to risk my own life for the things I believe in."

He opened his mouth, then closed it again. His eyes flicked over her face, lingered on the dampness of her tears. Then he turned away, leaning again on the windowsill, as if only the stone held him upright. Golden light from the setting sun caught his hair and made the wild fringe glow.

The silence drew out, tense and fraught with emotion, until Hannah felt tears welling again. "Are you so angry you won't even speak to me?" she whispered finally.

"No," he murmured. He turned back, a little unsteady on his feet, and caught himself against the stone. "I am… in awe." The slanting light caught his hollow cheeks and the curve of his lips in a smile she couldn't entirely decipher. "Forgive me. I am… not…" He blinked and shook his head, as if forcing back dizziness once again. "Not as eloquent as I wish to be. As you deserve." He rubbed one gloved hand over his face then let it drop, his fingers slack.

"Why don't you sit down?"

"I'm fine," he murmured.

"I'm not convinced that's true," Hannah said. She stepped closer, studying his face in the fading light. "What happened while I was gone? How long was it for you?"

Cadeyrn took a deep breath, then pushed himself upright and strode to the couch. Hannah watched him with wide eyes, convinced he would fall on his face at any moment. However, he managed to reach the couch and sat with as much dignity as he might have wished. "A few hours. Two. Three? I lost track. The duel was mostly magic; you wouldn't have seen much even if you had been there." He rubbed both hands over his face again, running them through his hair and leaving them clasped behind his neck.

"How do you feel? Do you need a doctor? Or a fairy doctor or something?"

He blinked slowly, as if the words were filtering through a haze of exhaustion before he could decipher them. "I *will be* fine. I feel…" He sighed heavily and pitched forward, suddenly boneless.

Hannah caught at his arm and succeeded only in pulling him slightly to the side and herself off balance, so that the two of them tumbled to the floor in an awkward jumble of limbs.

"Oh, Cadeyrn." Hannah brushed tears from her eyes. His eyes were closed, and his lips gleamed with the faint, thin sheen of silver blood, a little thicker in the corners of his mouth. Without thinking, she touched his face, cupping his cheek in her hand. His skin was smooth and warm, thin over the fine, hard cheekbone and jaw. She pulled back, and her fingers brushed his hair, wild and fine and soft as spidersilk.

He let out a long exhalation and half-mumbled something, then lapsed into disconcerting silence.

Hannah pressed the heels of her hands to her eyes and took a deep breath, letting it out slowly. *He'll be all right. He'll wake up, and he'll explain what's going on. I think I love him, but we need more time.*

A horrible thought nudged at her mind, and she pushed it away. Once, twice, and again. It became too insistent. *Why was the second scenario so vivid? Why would Einion lay out the betrayal so clearly? Was it an accident or intentional?*

Cadeyrn sucked in a breath and his eyes fluttered open. "I'm sorry," he muttered.

"Don't be," Hannah glared at him. "Just tell me the truth. What's wrong?"

Cadeyrn's eyes drifted closed, and took a deep, steadying breath. "Nothing permanent. Everything has consequences, Hannah." He sat up, a sudden effort that left him gasping. "I told you I broke a law when I broke the hold of the goblin fruit on you. My transgression had both magical consequences and legal repercussions. The physical toll is... intense." He closed his eyes and let his head rest against the edge of the velvet couch behind him. His spidersilk hair brushed Hannah's shoulder, and she restrained a sudden urge to run her hands through it. "For any other Fae, it would likely have been fatal. I am... stronger by blood and long training, but it was not easy. A magical duel immediately afterwards..." He gave a soft chuckle, lips twisting in a sardonic smile.

He let his head turn a little, studying her face. "You are troubled?" He closed his eyes again. "Forgive me. I was unkind in my anger." His crisp, elegant voice slurred.

"I'm not angry at you," Hannah said, trying to keep her voice soft. She slipped her hand into Cadeyrn's gloved one; he twitched in surprise before his fingers wrapped around hers. Through the thin leather of his glove she could feel the fine bones of his hand, the warmth and strength of his grip. "I was, but I'm not anymore."

"Thank you," he breathed, his eyes still closed. "I was right about you, you know. You are kind." He seemed to be drifting to sleep, his breathing deepening.

Hannah swallowed, chewing her lip, wondering whether she should wait or ask him now. "Cadeyrn, there's something I think you should know."

He sucked in a deep breath and swallowed. "What is it?" The shadows under his eyes made her heart constrict painfully.

"In the test, the second scenario with the traitor... it was much more vivid than the other two scenarios. Einion put a little of his own mind into the scenarios, didn't he?"

Cadeyrn straightened by force of will, his eyes focusing on her face with disconcerting intensity. "Go on," he murmured.

She licked her lips, trying to form the amorphous worry into words. "In the dream, if I can call it a dream, I believed I was the queen. But the kingdom was a blend of human and fairy. I suppose it had to be; the scenarios were from Einion's mind, but for me to make a choice that mattered, I still had to be me."

"Yes. You proved to be a remarkable queen." The pride shining in Cadeyrn's eyes caught Hannah by surprise. "Your decisions were wiser, perhaps, than I, or Einion, or even you would have made in real life, because you had the perspective of monarch, commoner, fairy, and human, all at once."

Hannah felt herself blushing. "I think he, perhaps by mistake, lent me some of his perspective and knowledge. The idea of a trusted subject and advisor being blackmailed into treason was much more vivid than the other two scenarios. The other choices were more... abstract, I suppose, or as if I were watching them secondhand, like in a movie. That one was something I lived."

Cadeyrn let out a soft breath. "You suspect there is truly such a traitor?"

"Yes." She swallowed hard. "I can wish Einion to tell me who it is, can't I?"

"I cannot ask you to use one of your wishes for that purpose, Hannah."

"You aren't asking me. I want to help. Would it work?"

He hesitated, then nodded. "Yes. He cannot lie, not while imprisoned as he is. He values his word, even while he is free."

Hannah gathered her courage and stood. At the table, she stared at the lamp for several seconds before brushing tentative fingers over the cool bronze surface.

"Einion? I have a wish."

Einion stood before her, his arms crossed. "What is it?" He glared at her.

Hannah licked her lips, considering her words carefully. "I wish to know if there is really a traitor in Cadeyrn's court, and if so, who it is."

"Yes. His Majesty Comonoc, king of the centaurs and ruler of the eastern hills, subject only to His Majesty

Cadeyrn, High King over all Seelie lands and peoples." Einion's words were clipped.

Out of the corner of her eye, Hannah saw Cadeyrn lurch to his feet.

"Is that all?" Einion ground out.

"Yes," Hannah breathed without looking at him, barely noticing as he vanished.

Cadeyrn was trembling. Without a word, he gestured, and the world turned inside out. Hannah staggered and nearly fell as the chaos resolved into the upper throne room.

Motionless, Comonoc stood in the center of the room, head bowed before the throne. With a wave of his hand, Cadeyrn lit the room, a thousand fairy lights casting a wash of cool light over the waiting centaur.

"Did he lie to me, or did you?" Cadeyrn whispered. "If you tell me it was him, I will believe you."

"I am a traitor, Your Majesty." Comonoc's voice was like the sighing of the wind through the dried leaves of a dying tree. "I await your judgement."

Cadeyrn rocked back on his heels, as if Comonoc had struck him. "Why?" His voice cracked.

"Tegwen, my beloved wife, was captured by Einion's forces four days ago." Comonoc murmured, his deep voice rumbling like distant thunder. "Not long after, the concussion of your magical feat, breaking the hold of goblin fruit upon the human child, rippled across our lands. Einion felt it but could not identify it at that distance. The price of Tegwen's life and freedom was an explanation of the concussion and his understanding of the opportunity to attack." Comonoc took a deep breath and let it out, the air trembling with emotion. "If Einion was true to his word, Tegwen is now free." He looked up, meeting Cadeyrn's gaze. "Einion, for all his malevolence, does value his word. I expect he has honored this promise."

Comonoc bowed his head again. "I outpaced him here, intending to warn you and die in your defense. I betrayed you for my wife, Your Majesty, but I never intended to live through it. I await your justice."

Fairylight glinted on the tears slipping down Cadeyrn's cheeks. His mouth opened, then closed, and he turned away without saying anything. He covered his face with both gloved hands.

Silence lay heavy upon them.

Comonoc's chest heaved with emotion, and finally he cried, in a voice that shook the stone beneath them, "Cadeyrn, my friend! Forgive me, and kill me! I have no wish to live after what I have done. Only look at me before you do it, and tell me you do not hate me."

Cadeyrn swayed and then steadied, his hands falling to his sides. He stood in front of the great centaur, a slight figure with wild hair and burning eyes. "I do not hate you, Comonoc. I could never hate you."

"Then I am satisfied. It is more than I deserve."

The Fae king licked his lips. "Let it be known that court is in session."

Comonoc bowed his head formally.

"Comonoc, you are charged with high treason. The penalty is death. How do you plead?"

"Guilty."

"So judged." Cadeyrn swayed, and Comonoc reached out a steadying hand to his shoulder.

"Wait…" Hannah breathed.

Cadeyrn looked at her. "Yes? What would you do, if you were queen?"

For a moment, Hannah imagined his tone was bitter, but then she heard only grief too great to bear, his throat tight with unshed tears.

She swallowed hysterical sobs, forcing herself to speak slowly. *Make the words count, Hannah.* "In the dream, the case was different. In this case, Comonoc wanted to defend you and your kingdom after his treason. Even if he'd meant to betray you, he turned away from it afterwards, and you know he never would have done it if he'd felt he had any choice."

Cadeyrn's bright gaze studied her face, but he said nothing.

She felt herself trembling, and she clenched her hands, her nails digging into her palms. She looked up at Comonoc's great face, his noble brow and the tears glinting on his cheeks. "Would Tegwen have wanted you to do this for her?"

He turned his face away. "No. She is braver than I. Perhaps it is for the best that I not have to face her and tell her of my crime."

"Comonoc has grown wiser," Hannah whispered. "Hasn't he? Do you think he would *ever* betray you again?"

Cadeyrn still said nothing, his eyes holding hers for long, silent moments. Finally his thin, pale lips curved in a faint smile. "Comonoc, you are pardoned."

The centaur blinked. "What? I don't understand."

"You have always been loyal. I choose to pardon you." Cadeyrn swayed and blinked, as if fighting dizziness, then said firmly, "I choose mercy. For our friendship. For the kingdom. And because in this case, I think mercy serves both honor and the kingdom better than the law does." He licked his lips. "There's no need to tell Tegwen."

Comonoc made a sudden, choked sound. "My wife will know of your mercy, Your Majesty. I thank you."

Cadeyrn murmured, "Speak not of it again, Comonoc. Let it not stand between us." He smiled, not a bitter smile but a flash of bright, determined joy.

Then he dropped like a puppet with his strings cut. Hannah half-caught him, staggering under his unexpected weight until Comonoc's great hands helped her ease Cadeyrn to the marble floor.

"Will he live?" Hannah whispered.

The centaur cleared his throat, but his voice was still tight. "Probably. He's tougher than he looks."

Hannah hesitated, then ran one finger over Cadeyrn's exaggerated eyebrows. The hairs were soft as down, his skin feverishly hot beneath her fingertips. "Is he always this hot?"

Comonoc blinked, then laid one huge hand over Cadeyrn's forehead. He frowned, then touched Hannah's forehead for comparison. "No, but humans are cooler than Fae. That is not what worries me."

The fairy king's hand clenched by his side, then relaxed.

"What worries you? What should we do?"

Comonoc's deep voice was unexpectedly soft. "Did he eat last night? Or this morning?"

"This morning, yes. Not last night."

"Then let him sleep."

"On the floor?" Hannah had a feeling of unreality; Cadeyrn's face was as white as the marble he lay on, his dark hair wild around his head.

"Better than moving him." The centaur covered his face with both hands; his chest heaved as if he were weeping, but he made no sound.

A soft hoot caught Hannah's attention, and she gasped when she saw Cara hunched miserably some distance away. The owl held one wing away from his body;

47

it hung at an unnatural angle, and there was a spot of red blood on the white feathers.

"Oh, Cara!" She held out a tentative hand. Cara glared at her with baleful eyes, then reluctantly hopped toward Cadeyrn, pointedly ignoring Hannah. The owl climbed onto Cadeyrn's chest, talons digging through his shirt into his skin. Cadeyrn's breath caught, and the owl screeched into his face.

The Fae king's eyes fluttered open, and he twitched a hand. Cara squawked in surprise. He flapped his wings experimentally, hooted softly, and shuffled his feet. Hannah's eyes widened when she realized that his wing was healed. Cadeyrn's eyes were closed again, his breathing more even.

Hannah glanced at Comonoc. The centaur didn't seem to notice the tear streaks on his cheeks.

He rumbled, "I will stand guard. Stay with him, human child."

FOUR

Hannah sat by Cadeyrn for hours. For a long time she watched him breathe; he had a worrying tendency to gasp silently for breath at odd intervals, as if the air had suddenly ceased to fill his lungs. After a while, she realized those intervals were growing longer, and her worry eased. The light from the windows faded, but the fairy lights remained bright and cool above them.

Her eyes gritty and her stomach rumbling, she finally lay beside Cadeyrn on the floor, one arm curled beneath her head. She rested the tips of her fingers on his gloved wrist so that she would feel his movement when he woke, and finally drifted into dreams.

Warm light across her face brought Hannah slowly into wakefulness. Her eyes still closed, she pondered the ache in her shoulder and her neck before realizing that the floor was hard and her arm was asleep. She groaned as she shifted, still half-asleep.

"Why are you on the floor?" Cadeyrn whispered.

She blinked at him blearily. "Uh... you were here? I didn't know how to get you back to your bed, and..." She let her voice trail away as she studied his face.

He was smiling at her as if she had said something strange and wonderful. With a slight gesture of his hand, Hannah found herself sitting on the couch in Cadeyrn's sitting room. He sat at the other end of the couch; only his almost unnatural stillness gave the lie to his relaxed posture.

"You are remarkable," he murmured.

Hannah felt her cheeks heat. *I'm too sleepy for compliments. What should I say?* No words were required. He gestured, and breakfast appeared on the nearby table. When she looked back at him, he was asleep.

THE DAY WAS QUIET. Cadeyrn slept deeply. Only now did Hannah notice that the wound on his hip had bled at some point in the last day, though the silver blood soaked into his trousers was already dried and flaking away. He ate neither breakfast nor lunch; when the sun was overhead she ate the remains of breakfast.

She studied the bronze lamp in the middle of the table, careful not to touch it. It looked old fashioned, as if Cadeyrn, in making it, had tapped into her imagination of what a genie-prison ought to look like. Something from Arabian nights, full of wonder and danger and incense-scented magic.

Hannah hesitated at the door to Cadeyrn's room, then stepped inside. She walked through his bookshelves again, marveling at the collection. The aisles seemed intimate, the wood of the shelves dark with age and use. She found a reading nook at the end of one aisle with a worn leather armchair and a matching ottoman. A table by one arm had a stack of books on it, none in languages she recognized. Continuing onward, she realized that the aisles had begun to curve and entwine at odd angles, and she had gone up and down several staircases. A twist of nerves made her suddenly glance back, reminding herself of the way. But the unfamiliarity of the endless library could not make her nervous for long. Cadeyrn's presence filled the space.

Finally she found a section of books in English and smiled to see shelves of her favorites. She choose two, a classic and a book by an author she'd never heard of, and found her way back to the bedroom, then to the sitting room.

Cadeyrn was awake.

"I... I HOPE YOU DON'T MIND." Hannah held up the books, feeling herself blushing furiously. "I thought I might read a bit, since you were sleeping."

"Not at all," he murmured. His eyes swept over her, and he smiled faintly. "I offered you the kingdom. I could hardly begrudge you a few books from my library."

She swallowed a lump in her throat. "How are you feeling?"

"Well enough." He stood, wavered a moment, then steadied, and strode to the window. He looked out into the sunset.

She frowned. "Does your palace move? I thought the sunrise was out that window."

He turned to her, his eyes sparkling. "You've noticed!"

"I thought I must be mistaken." She found herself grinning. "Does it really move?"

"Why not? It's magic." He gestured, and she stepped closer to stand shoulder to shoulder with him, looking at the lush valley below. "It doesn't go any distance, but the hallways shift. Rooms move. It likes to surprise me with the view."

Hannah blinked. "It's sentient?"

He glanced at her, a secretive smile tugging at his lips. "Not exactly. But it has a personality. It's mischievous but not malicious. It likes to help and to play. It's like a child, I suppose."

"Or a goblin?"

He snorted softly. "I should hope not. I'd never find anything if that were the case."

She took a deep breath, breathing in his faint scent of moonlight and frost and magic.

The silence lengthened.

Vermillion streaks lit the sky, competing with deep blue and gold and crimson and an astonishing, brilliant orange. Almost lost in the haze of distance she saw the ragged edges of mountains, and a glint of blue-gold.

"What's that?"

"A waterfall." He sighed and folded his arms, leaning back against the stone. She wondered if he meant to look so graceful and elegant, or whether it came naturally to him. "I'd take you, but perhaps it would be a more pleasant journey after I've had a night's sleep." He glanced at her. "You'd think I hadn't slept all day."

Hannah looked out the window again. The light gilded the distant trees and the nearer roads, large stone buildings and smaller thatched houses. "Is that where the goblins live?"

He glanced out the window and shook his head. "Most of them are on the other side. These houses are mostly those of the imps, hobgoblins, and brownies. The pixies are just over there. Most of them live outside of town, though. They like their space."

The fading light caught his affectionate smile for a moment, and Hannah's heart stuttered. *Does he know he's beautiful?* He gestured absently, and fairy lights blinked into being, filling the space above them with a thousand pinpricks of light.

"What are you thinking?" he asked, his head tilted a little in that strange-yet-familiar manner.

She searched for words and then discarded them. "I knew you were a good king. From the beginning, I knew that. But I don't think I really understood what that meant until now."

Cadeyrn took a deep breath and let it out, his eyes searching her face. "Thank you, Hannah." He licked his lips, opened his mouth as if he meant to say something else, and then changed his mind. He bowed gracefully to kiss her hand, his lips just barely grazing her knuckles and his hand hot through the thin leather of his glove. Hannah blushed furiously; when he glanced up at her and noticed, his eyes sparkled a little.

"Do you realize that embarrasses me?" she breathed.

"Why?" he asked, his voice all innocence and seduction and velvet.

Because it's chivalrous and impossibly sexy and how dare you pretend that you don't realize my heart is going a thousand beats a minute and I'm getting weak-kneed just looking at you. "Um…" She swallowed.

His fingers slipped from hers. "It is a gesture of respect, Hannah." The sparkle in his eyes faded into resignation. "I hold you in the highest respect. I had hoped for… more, but even now, I had thought that a gesture of respect would not be too unwelcome. I beg your pardon." He turned back to the window, focusing on the horizon.

"Cadeyrn, that's not what I meant," she whispered.

A muscle in his jaw twitched, and he closed his eyes as if preparing himself for something unpleasant. "In what way have I misunderstood you?" Despite the words, his tone was gentle; with a distant part of her mind, she marveled at his self-control.

"It's just unusual." She licked her lips. "It's old-fashioned. It makes me feel like a princess, like I'm playing a role meant for someone else. I don't know the script."

He turned to look at her, eyebrows drawn downward in an inquisitive frown. "Why would feeling like a princess embarrass you?" He leaned against the stone wall, alarmingly pale, his eyes intent on hers.

"Because I'm *not* a princess. I'm an ordinary human girl... woman... who has a job and a little house and a decade-old car."

He murmured, "You are far from ordinary." He licked his lips, and added, "I would kiss your hand again, to make the point, but I fear you would see it as disrespectful, rather than as I intend it."

Kiss me! "I wouldn't mind so much," she whispered.

Something in his eyes flickered, and the air seemed alive with tension. Her heart in her throat, she reached out to clasp his hand in hers again, threading her fingers between his.

His voice tight, he whispered, "I don't want to misunderstand you, Hannah. What do you wish of me?"

The word *wish*, the veiled hope in his eyes... Hannah found herself unable to speak for a moment. So she closed her eyes and brought Cadeyrn's gloved hand to her cheek, feeling the warmth, the almost imperceptible trembling, the smoothness of the leather against her skin.

Her eyes still closed, she whispered, "I wish you'd kiss me. I wish—"

His lips pressed against hers, and she couldn't breathe for the *spark* that arched her back, a sudden rush of desire and emotion that caught her breath in her lungs and brought her thoughts to a standstill. Time shattered, and she didn't care.

Cadeyrn pulled away, his arm braced on the stone wall. He was breathing hard, his breath warm against her hair, his own wild hair brushing the sensitive skin of her neck as he sagged against the wall.

A sudden thought curled sick within her belly, and she whispered, "You didn't do that because I made you, did I? Can a wish do that?"

His soft laughter startled her. "No, Hannah. Wishes cannot compel love, and love is what you felt."

She rested her cheek against his, feeling his breath against her ear, his hair tickling her face.

"What else do you wish, Hannah?" His whisper was so soft she nearly thought she imagined it.

She couldn't speak for the emotion that nearly choked her. After a moment, she felt Cadeyrn's lean body sag a little more against the stone, as if hope alone had held him up. He barely touched her, only his left shoulder against hers, his cheek against hers, his forehead resting against the wall.

"Come sit, Cadeyrn," she whispered. "You're tired."

"I'm fine," she imagined him saying, though the words were only an indistinct murmur. But he straightened, his shoulders square and strong. She couldn't quite tell whether he brushed his lips across her hair as he turned; she found herself wishing that he had.

CADEYRN WAVED A HAND at the table and produced an exquisite meal, along with several books at the other end of the table. He held out her chair for her, then slid her chair forward. Hannah looked down at her hands clenched in her lap, at how the skin stretched tight over her knuckles. *I wish I knew how to say the things I feel.* She looked up to see Cadeyrn leaning both hands on the table, his nostrils flaring as he fought to keep his breathing even.

"What happened?" She stood. "What can I do to help?"

"Nothing. It will pass."

Long minutes later, he breathed more easily, and he sat across from her without a word. The circles under his eyes seemed deeper, his cheeks a little thinner, but perhaps that was merely the cool light of the fairy lights above.

Or perhaps not. After eating a moment in silence, Hannah looked up to see Cadeyrn resting his elbow on the arm of the chair, his hand covering his eyes.

He was asleep.

AN HOUR AFTER she'd finished eating, long after the sunset had faded, Cadeyrn woke, walked her to her room, and bid her goodnight. She couldn't read his expression, aside from bone-deep weariness, and she hesitated, but finally said, "Cadeyrn?"

"Yes, dearest Hannah?"

She swallowed. "Will you get better?"

His teeth flashed, and she was momentarily reminded of her nerves that first evening, at his sharp-toothed smile, that crackle of danger and power in the air around him. "Yes, dearest Hannah." His smile faded, and he murmured. "Tomorrow I will have the strength to take you to your home."

"I'm not so concerned about that." She licked her lips and gathered her courage, then raised her hand to touch his cheek, running one thumb across the shadow under his eye. He stood still as stone, as if afraid to move lest she pull away. His eyelashes were so soft she could barely feel them brushing her skin. "I was just worried about you."

His eyebrows drew downward in a faint frown. "I… hadn't thought that causing you worry would be so pleasant. I think I'm a bit ashamed of that."

She couldn't help a smile. His eyes sparkled in response, making her heart flutter against her ribs. "Well, see that you don't do it again," she managed.

"Don't worry. I've threatened the goblins with a very unpleasant demise if they try anything so ridiculous in the future." His smile glinted in the dim light, wild and fey and, despite his words, kind. *He's kind*, she thought wonderingly. *Despite what his father did, how he was treated, he's so very kind, and far more gentle than he has any reason to be.*

She swallowed a lump in her throat. *I think I love you, Cadeyrn.* "Goodnight, Cadeyrn."

"Goodnight, dearest Hannah."

FIVE

A messenger came the next morning while they were eating breakfast by the window. A tiny yellow and black bird flew to Cadeyrn and chattered at him.

He frowned. "Tell them I will be there momentarily."

The bird flew away. Hannah had a disturbing sense of deja vu. The last messenger, Comonoc, had not brought good tidings. The tightness of Cadeyrn's lips told her he was concerned as well, though he smiled at her with his customary courtesy.

"A delegation from the Unseelie court requests an audience with me." He studied her. "You may attend if you wish, but I will advise you to say nothing. Besides the danger inherent in conversing with an Unseelie, there is protocol to be observed."

She nodded.

Hannah followed him into the hallway and down a short corridor before finding the throne room. *This isn't how we got here before.* Her wonder at the changing hallways was quickly lost in marveling at Cadeyrn himself. He stopped before a door and produced a magnificent green cloak from thin air, swirling it around his shoulders with a careless grace and fastening it with a clasp set with an enormous green gemstone set in gold. With a wave of his hand, his casual breeches had shifted into a finer fabric of deep brown; his blue shirt became darker and more severe, outlining his slim, hard figure. A crown appeared on his head, a simple band of hammered gold an inch wide; his wild hair stuck up, setting off the rich metal.

Cadeyrn gave her a quick glance, and she had the feeling he was debating whether to change her clothes as well. He must have decided not to, because he raised his chin and strode into the throne room.

The door opened behind the throne this time. Cadeyrn's footsteps sounded sharp and commanding as he strode to the front of the dias to stand in front of the marble throne. Hannah followed, stepping just inside the room and stopping with her back to the wall.

The Unseelie delegation comprised three fairies, all pale and unnaturally beautiful, just as Einion was. Their hair ranged from gold to dark brown, and their attire was splendid, though not quite as luxurious as Cadeyrn's robe.

Comonoc stepped forward from the shadows and bowed deeply to Cadeyrn. "Your Majesty High King Cadeyrn, I present Hywel, Aneirin, and Iorwerth, provincial kings of the Unseelie under His Majesty Einion, and designated speakers for all Unseelie peoples in this matter."

"Thank you, Comonoc," Cadeyrn glanced at him and nodded. "Welcome to the Seelie Court, Your Majesties. What brings you here now?"

The three kings bowed gracefully, and Hywell stepped forward. He had pale gold eyes in a fine-boned face. His expression was serious, with no hint of humor.

"Your Majesty High King Cadeyrn, we pay our respects." He bowed again, more deeply this time. "We have come to make an unusual request. Your subject, the human Hannah, bested our king His Majesty Einion. She holds his wishes. We ask that you order her to use one of those wishes to compel him to renounce his authority as king. As payment, we offer her two wishes, one to replace that which she uses to compel him, and another as payment for doing so." Hywell's eyes were bright and hard.

"Hannah is not my subject, and she will make her own decisions. However, I will advise her." He glanced over his shoulder at her and nodded her forward.

Hannah stepped to his side, feeling her stomach churning with nerves. Cadeyrn murmured in her ear, "Be *very* careful with your words, Hannah." He waited until she nodded before he straightened.

Her mouth dry, Hannah asked, "Why do you ask this? Do you want to be free of his rule? Is he a bad king?"

Hywell blinked, and Hannah had the disconcerting feeling that her question was not at all what he had expected. "No," he said carefully. "No, he *was* a very good king, by our reckoning. But it seems likely that he will be imprisoned for a long time." His eyes focused on her with unnerving intensity. "At least, if I were in your place in the Seelie Court, advised by His Majesty High King Cadeyrn, it would be centuries before he was free again." His expression was unexpectedly bleak.

Hannah chewed her lip and glanced at Cadeyrn. He gave her a faint, encouraging smile, so she ventured, "But why do you want him to renounce his kingship?"

Hywell glanced at Cadeyrn, then said, "Our lands are under attack. The Shadows ventured forth shortly after the end of the challenge which concluded with His Majesty Einion's imprisonment. We cannot effectively defend ourselves without the power invested in him. We also have made allies that are... unreliable, at best, when we are weak."

Cadeyrn nodded. "I understand."

Hannah took a deep breath. "I don't."

Hywell's gaze flicked between them. "You are human? You have no knowledge of magic or fairy law?"

"Right," she said, careful of her words.

"A fairy king is far, far more powerful than his subjects. Part of this is a result of the enchantment during the crowning ceremony, and part is a result of his connection with the land and the peoples he rules. The formal investiture of royalty with the consent of the people is a spell cast by the whole people acting in concert. Also, a king is often among the strongest of his people even before he is crowned, but the strength bestowed upon him as king is almost unrelated to this.

"His Majesty High King Cadeyrn and His Majesty Einion are the two most powerful kings by far, and, in honesty, His Majesty High King Cadeyrn outclasses His Majesty Einion in personal magic as well as the extent of his rule, but His Majesty Einion is both powerful and clever. Both have several kings under them who have authority over peoples or lands."

Hywell sighed. "While it is not unheard of for a fairy to be imprisoned, it is quite rare. A high king has never been imprisoned. His Majesty Einion remains king of his people, and the power of the kingship resides in him. Yet while bound, he cannot defend us or our lands.

"In other circumstances when a king becomes unable to serve, he can be deposed and an heir can take power. But this will not work for two reasons. First, Einion has not named an heir, so his power would not transfer upon his deposition. Second, just as he is prevented from taking action while sealed away, others cannot take action against him, including deposing him.

"Our only hope is for you to compel him to renounce his throne, despite the lack of a clear heir, and hope that the resulting power struggle is brief and relatively bloodless, so the new king will grow in power quickly enough to take up the fight and prevent the Shadows overrunning us all." Hywell's clear explanation had ended in a clipped tone of frustration.

Hannah licked her lips. "I'd like to think about it until tomorrow." She glanced at Cadeyrn. "Is that all right?"

Cadeyrn nodded, the picture of gracious courtesy, and addressed the kings. "Consider yourselves my guests until tomorrow morning. We will give you an answer then." He gestured, and three imps appeared in the far doorway, beckoning the fairy monarchs.

"Yes, Your Majesty. Thank you." Hywell bowed again, and they withdrew, following the imps into the hall.

Cadeyrn led Hannah back to his suite before saying a word. He gestured toward the couch, and Hannah sat, watching with wide eyes as Cadeyrn removed the luxurious cloak and made it disappear, along with the emerald clasp and the gold crown.

"Is your crown real gold?"

He pulled it back out of thin air and handed it to her. "Yes."

The weight startled her; he'd handled it as if it weighed nothing.

"It's old," he said absently, studying the bronze lamp on the table. "Several millennia. Einion's is around the same age." He sat on the couch and rubbed both hands over his face, glancing up when she handed the crown back to him. He slid it into the air again and it disappeared.

Hannah thought about what Hywell had said. "What are the Shadows?" she asked.

Cadeyrn frowned, his exaggerated eyebrows drawing downward. "We don't know. They're not of Faerie, but their world intersects ours... sometimes. They make advances into Faerie lands at long intervals.

"They're best fought with magic. Light-embued swords are effective. They haven't ventured into Seelie lands since I was very young, so I have limited knowledge of them."

Hannah considered, turning the question of Einion's freedom over in her mind. "I think I need to talk to Einion in order to make a decision."

Silence drew out while Cadeyrn thought, and Hannah studied him surreptitiously. His skin was still horribly pale, and his gloved hand shook a little as he absently rubbed his jaw.

"Can he lie to me?" she asked.

"No, not exactly. Not while bound as he is. Even when he was free, Einion was not given to outright lies... he was too clever for that and preferred to mislead. He can still mislead you or trick you to some extent, though less perhaps than while he was free. He will likely try to get you to say 'I wish' or get you to agree that something is your wish. He will then 'grant it' and be one wish closer to freedom." He took a deep breath and Hannah had the impression that he was fighting dizziness. "He doesn't have to answer your questions or converse with you at all except as necessary to fairly evaluate a wish. He *can*, but he may choose not to, and that is his right."

Hannah nodded. "All right."

Cadeyrn stood, his feet set wide and his arms folded across his chest. "Be cautious, then." He nodded toward the lamp.

Her fingers trembled as she brushed them over the lamp. "Einion, we need to talk."

The world shifted and he appeared, standing a few feet from her. "What is it?" He glanced at Cadeyrn and his eyes narrowed, his gaze flicking up and down, back to Cadeyrn's face. "How long has it been?" he breathed. "A week?"

"Two days," Cadeyrn said, his voice neutral.

Einion blinked. "You're recovering well, after ripping the world apart at its seams. I admit I am impressed." He turned to Hannah with a sharp-toothed smile. "Now then, what did you wish to talk about?"

"I…" Hannah stopped and glared at him. "I'm not making a wish! If and when I wish something, I will clearly and unmistakably state that I am doing so. If you assume a wish when one is not so stated, I will take it that you are cheating on your penalty. I assume there are consequences to that, although I have no idea what they might be."

Einion paled, and he murmured, "I understand very clearly."

Hannah chewed her lip, and Einion regained his composure.

"I am not bound to converse with you for your amusement," he said. "If you have a wish, state it clearly, and if you have no wish, explain to me why I should attend you." His lip curled in frustration.

"We…" She glanced at Cadeyrn, who merely smiled back neutrally, "Well, His Majesty High King Cadeyrn received a petition this morning from your subjects. They asked him to make me compel you to renounce your throne so that they can choose a new king."

Einion's eyes widened. "Why?" he breathed.

"They're being attacked by the Shadows," she said, feeling suddenly uncertain. *What are the Shadows anyway?*

The Unseelie king spun on his heel and took a few steps away, pulling up short as if yanked back by an invisible force. He didn't seem to care, spinning to pace in a different direction, his face white with rage. He ground out something indecipherable; Hannah had the feeling that if she had understood his language, she would have heard some obscenity.

"It wouldn't help," he said, his words sharp with anger, though more controlled now. "I haven't designated an heir. There would be a bloodbath, and the Shadows would take too much ground. Even if the factions *wanted* to unite, they couldn't consolidate their power fast enough. Then the new king would have to learn how to wield his power; the Shadows would slaughter him, and those under him." Einion trembled with impotent rage. "Even if I voluntarily renounced my throne, it wouldn't help."

He paced again and Hannah watched him warily. The air crackled; he was lightning waiting to strike.

Blue eyes flicked to her face. "You could free me. Use your wishes! Whatever you want, it's yours. Wealth, fame…love?" He smiled mirthlessly, and behind the sharp teeth she saw his desperation.

What do I want? Out of the corner of her eye, she saw Cadeyrn's white face, the sharp line of his jaw. *Could he compel someone to love me?*

Hannah's voice shook a little. "I don't think it works that way. I think you're trying to trick me. I don't think you could deliver love. Love is a choice. And even if you could… that would be horrible."

"You explicitly said I could not try to twist your words into a wish if you did not mean to make a wish. But there is no law that I use *magic* to grant a wish, or even that I have any hand in making the wish come true." Einion's face was bleak. "I hoped you would wish Cadeyrn to love you, and I could proclaim your wish fulfilled."

"Wouldn't that be cheating?" Hannah whispered.

"I am desperate!" he hissed. "And not for myself. I recall you have a history of mercy in such cases."

Hannah stepped closer to Cadeyrn and murmured, "I'm not sure I have two wishes that I'm ready to make right now. I think… it seems like making a wish without real need would be unwise. Maybe even unsafe."

"You are right; it would not be entirely safe. Einion cannot seek revenge against you." Cadeyrn spoke in a low voice, but Hannah realized with surprise that he had not sealed them in silence as he had on the Dueling Ground. "But he was already set upon attacking the Seelie through me. When free, he would be permitted to continue that course of action. I would guess that he would take action against the Shadows first; he is, after all, a good king to his people, at least by Unseelie reckoning. I am not as weak as I was, but I am not yet fully recovered. I may be able to stand against Einion. I may not." His eyes flashed dangerously. "I would assuredly make his victory difficult, but this would be his best opportunity to attack if he had the freedom and inclination to do so."

Hannah pondered that.

Einion paced away and back, stopping to clasp his hands behind his back. "While freeing me is *perhaps* dangerous, keeping me imprisoned under these circumstances is *certainly* dangerous. While I cannot seek revenge upon Hannah for my own imprisonment, I *could* seek vengeance if my people suffer when they could have been helped." His chest heaved, and he said, "I *will* get free someday! Even if the lamp is cast into the bottom of the sea with a wish remaining, or two, in thousands or tens of thousands of years something will destroy it or someone will wish on it. Do you think I would not remember the destruction of my people or the pain they suffered? I could seek vengeance on Seelie and humans alike. No matter if you," he focused on Hannah, "are long dead. I could seek vengeance upon your children, your descendants, your entire species."

Hannah met his cold glare. "What if I used one of my two remaining wishes to have you preserve the lamp against anything that might destroy it? How long might you stay imprisoned then?"

He paled, and his nostrils flared. He trembled and stared at her for a long moment, his face tight and hard. He said nothing, only pacing with quick, agitated steps away and back, away and back again.

Cadeyrn murmured in Hannah's ear, "This might be the first time in history that a fairy king has been frightened by the same person twice." She glanced at him and found his expression unreadable. Amusement, perhaps. Caution, both of her and for her. *I don't want him to be afraid.* The idea of Cadeyrn fearing her caused a horrible twist in her belly, and she took a steadying breath. *I want to be the kind of person he can trust.*

"Could I wish him to defend his people from the Shadows?" she whispered to Cadeyrn.

"No. Your control is over him as an individual, not his office as a king. You cannot apply the entire power of the Unseelie people by your wishes. While bound, he cannot apply it either."

"Could I free him just while the Shadows are attacking?"

"No. If you free him, he is free."

Hannah watched Einion. He hadn't argued with any of what Cadeyrn had said; since he couldn't lie, his silence was an admission that Cadeyrn was right.

"I think I know you better than you think I do. Maybe better than anyone else does. You showed me your heart when you gave me the dreams, although I don't think you meant to. If I ask for your word not to attack Cadeyrn, me, humans, or Seelie ever again in exchange for my releasing you now, would you give it? It may be the only hope for your people."

Einion stared at her. He licked his lips, sharp teeth flashing, then said carefully, "I am a fairy. I am *Unseelie*. I cannot change my nature, even if I would. You cannot ask a cat to be a dog or a fish. But, as much as it is in my power, if you free me, knowing what you know, I and my people will be in your debt. We honor our debts." He hesitated, then added, "I am not sure that my idea of a friend is the same as yours, but I, as Einion and as king of the Unseelie, would be forever your friend."

Hannah looked at Cadeyrn. He gazed back at her, his expression open but neutral. She *wished* he would tell her what to do, what would be best... but she said nothing, only watched as his eyes softened. *He trusts me. But what do I do?*

She formed the words in her head, turning them around and looking for weaknesses before she opened her mouth. "Based on your word, I free you from your imprisonment in the lamp."

Einion's eyes flashed. "Cadeyrn, if you do not make her your queen, you are a fool." He vanished before the sound of his voice died away.

She was trembling, and she didn't realize it until Cadeyrn stood in front of her, clasping her shaking hands. "You have either made the most astonishing and unexpected allies, or a *spectacularly* unwise choice… I have no idea which. But it was a noble thing to do either way, and I think the tale will be told long after every other event of this age is forgotten."

SIX

C lose your eyes."

Cadeyrn's gloved fingers wrapped around hers, and she felt the world fall away and reassemble itself. The transition was nearly as smooth as it had been that first time, and she smiled to think that Cadeyrn was nearly recovered.

The familiar sight of her living room greeted her. The worn couch and once-used fireplace now seemed strangely foreign. *It's all so prosaic.* Her heart beat wildly, and she turned to Cadeyrn.

"Stay for a while?" Her voice shook, and she cleared her throat. "I could make cookies or something."

He let out a breath, as if he'd been holding it, wondering what she would say. "I've never made cookies the normal way."

She blinked. "Never?"

He shook his head.

Making cookies was both surreal and comforting. Cadeyrn watched as she assembled the ingredients and measured the butter, sugar, vanilla, flour, and everything else. Brushing by him to get out the mixer, she inhaled the faint scent of moonlight, frost, and the alien strength of him, the ozone after a lightning strike, a cold spiciness that made her tingle. She wished he'd kiss her again, but she swallowed the words.

Her hand on the spatula, she said, "This is loud," then turned on the mixer. She was glad she'd warned him; he tensed, and the air crackled around him with barely restrained power.

With the mixing done, she started spooning drop cookies onto a cookie sheet, glancing up at Cadeyrn's face. "Do you want to do this?"

"If you wish," he murmured. His gloved hand was warm as he took the spoon from her.

"You might get dough on your gloves. Don't you want to take them off?" she asked.

He glanced up at her, blue eyes bright and unreadable. "Do you wish it?"

"Not a *wish*..." she bit her lip. "I just want you to be comfortable with me. You don't have to hide."

He paused, and for an instant she thought his expression was gratitude, or perhaps wonder, or maybe it was something else. Then he murmured, "Magic cleans leather rather well, actually. But," he peeled off the gloves, revealing his marble-white skin crossed by ink-black scars, "I appreciate your thoughtfulness." He placed the gloves off to the side and studied his hands, his lips tight with disdain, then looked up. "Besides, I have a request of my own when we are finished."

"What is it?" Hannah asked curiously.

Cadeyrn held her gaze. "It is proper for me to visit your parents and request their permission to court you. Since you have given me some hope of a successful suit, I would like to meet your parents and then begin."

A funny sound escaped before Hannah found her voice. "I thought you had begun already. I mean... you *proposed*!" She found herself struggling to suppress giggles.

Cadeyrn winced and gave her a reproachful look. "I wasn't thinking clearly. My intent has not changed, but I beg your forgiveness for my lapse in courtesy. It was premature, as I acknowledged at the time." He glanced away, and Hannah realized, with some disbelief, that he was *blushing*; faint silver-pink glowed on his sharp cheekbones.

She forced down the giggles and slipped her hands around his, feeling the faint texture of the branching scars, the calluses on his palms and the pads of his fingers. "I'm teasing you, Cadeyrn. You have nothing to ask forgiveness for." She rubbed one finger over his knuckles, considering her words, then blushed as she realized what she was doing. "We can start driving as soon as the cookies are done."

"That's easy," he said, waving a hand. "Must we drive?"

Hannah looked in the oven and grinned at the perfectly done cookies. "My parents would think it strange if we showed up on their doorstep with no car. Besides, you aren't tired of me yet, are you?"

"Not at all." His gentle smile made her heart beat faster, and she let her hair fall over her face, hiding her heated cheeks.

THEY SMILED at each other over milk and cookies, then packed the rest in freezer bags for her parents.

Hannah called ahead. "I'm coming for the weekend, if that's all right. I'm bringing a friend." Out of the corner of her eye, she saw Cadeyrn's startled smile, as if the word *friend* had been an unexpected gift.

The drive was quiet. Hannah glanced at Cadeyrn at intervals as the minutes and hours passed. The roads were salted and clear, and tiny snow flurries eddied across the interstate.

Once they exited the interstate, Cadeyrn watched the houses passing by with apparent interest, a faint smile flickering over his lips as if the human dwellings both fascinated and amused him.

"What do they know of me?" Cadeyrn asked when they were only a few minutes from Hannah's parents' house. "Anything?"

"They know I used to have a pen pal. That's about it. They never saw your letters." Hannah swallowed. "Will you tell them you're a fairy?"

"I would prefer to be entirely honest and open with them."

"I... maybe you shouldn't talk about it." At his gently raised eyebrow, she added, "Fairies are pretty much mythical. No one really believes you exist."

Cadeyrn frowned slightly. "I will not make it my first topic of conversation, if you wish, but I will not lie to them. If we are to be wed, I will not do so under false pretenses."

Hannah took a deep breath, feeling the cool, dry air sting her lungs. "That's fair."

THE ROADS NEAR Hannah's parents' house were lined with dirty ridges of snow pushed up by snow plows, and she navigated the streets carefully in the already-fading light. Pulling into the familiar driveway, she said, "That's the tree I used to climb." She gestured at the massive oak in the otherwise open front yard. "I helped my mom plant a bunch of flowers in those beds a few years ago; I think I wrote about that."

Cadeyrn nodded. Hannah wondered if he was nervous. His clothes were unwrinkled and crisp, despite the three hour drive, and Hannah found herself feeling rumpled and tired beside him. She pushed the feeling aside and led him to the door.

"Come on in," she said, feeling a sudden rush of emotion. How many times had she thought about her fairy pen pal, wishing that he could experience the warmth of a kind family like hers? She remembered lines from his letters over the years, and her eyes welled with sudden tears.

Father was angry again. My swordplay is quite good for my age, or so my tutor says, but Father was not satisfied. I wish he would beat me again; it would be easier to bear than the words he cut me with this time.

Mother has gone to visit friends, leaving me alone with my lessons and Father's disappointment. I pray your summer is more gentle.

I have learned a hard lesson in trust. Comonoc is a true friend, though he is closer to my father's age than my own. The others revere my father's cleverness and discipline, but see kindness as weakness. Perhaps they are right, and I am a disappointment.

"What is wrong, dearest Hannah?" Cadeyrn asked. "You are unhappy."

She swallowed the lump in her throat. "I… used to wish you could come visit me and see what a family was supposed to be like. I wanted you to know what it felt like to be loved."

He let out a soft breath, his eyes warm. "Oh, Hannah. I thank you." He hesitated, then raised his hand to brush a strand of hair back from her face, the tips of his gloved fingers lingering on her temple. "Your kindness is a gift I had not truly hoped for."

I wish you would kiss me! Hannah leaned her cheek against his hand for a moment, knowing that his smile widened, then pulled away only to slip her hand in his and draw him into the kitchen.

"Mom? Dad? This is my friend Cadeyrn."

Her mom looked up from the stove. "Oh! I'm so sorry I didn't hear you come in. It's so very nice to meet you. Cadeyrn, is it?" She stumbled over the unfamiliar name. "I'm Karen." She removed the oven mitt from her hand and held it out. Her eyes widened when Cadeyrn clasped her hand in his gloved one and bent gracefully to kiss her hand.

"I'm Dave. I've... not heard much about you, actually, so it will be nice to hear about you over dinner." Hannah's father shook Cadeyrn's hand with agreeable vigor.

"Can I do anything to help, Mom?" Hannah offered.

"Oh, no, honey. Dinner is ready. I was just getting the brownies in the oven." She motioned everyone into the little dining room, where the plates were set and serving dishes already full.

"Did you enjoy your cruise?" Hannah asked. Cadeyrn seated her before he sat himself, and Hannah noticed her parents noticing the unusual courtesy. *I wonder if he realizes it's unusual.*

"Oh, it was wonderful!" After a quick blessing of the food, Karen and Dave spent a few minutes telling about the nightly dancing in the ballroom and the fancy food, the snorkeling and the swimming with dolphins.

"And now tell us about yourself, Cadeyrn." Karen smiled warmly at her guest. "What do you do? How did you meet Hannah?"

"I… have a position with many responsibilities. I've been asked not to speak too much about it." He shifted topics smoothly. "I've been corresponding with Hannah for quite some time, but we only met in person a few weeks ago, just before Christmas."

Karen shot a glance at Dave and frowned slightly. "So… you work for the government?" she asked tentatively.

"… Not *your* government." He frowned and glanced at Hannah. "I actually came to speak with you about Hannah. Although she is of age, and quite capable of making her own decisions, I wish to show my respect for her, and for you, by formally requesting your consent to court her. In time, with her consent and yours, I wish to make her my wife."

Karen and Dave glanced at each other.

Dave cleared his throat. "Well, that's very… old-fashioned… of you. Not in a bad way! I'm… it's a good start." He nodded thoughtfully, studying Cadeyrn with sharp eyes. "But I'm not particularly keen on my daughter marrying a foreign spy, or whatever it is you do."

"I'm not a spy." Cadeyrn said seriously, though the corners of his lips turned up as if the idea were amusing. "Hannah will always be free to visit whenever she wishes, even after our wedding, should she accept my proposal."

"How did you meet Hannah, exactly?" Dave asked.

"We have been exchanging letters for many years. Since we were both children, in fact. At last, when Hannah wished it, we met. I had not…" Cadeyrn licked his lips, "I had expected to enjoy meeting an old friend for the first time. I had not expected her to be so entrancingly beautiful, nor to so quickly see proof of her kindness. Her gentleness won my heart, and her wisdom was additional proof that she would be a fit partner in my responsibilities."

Karen couldn't help smiling at his courtly words. "Come, Hannah. Help me get the brownies ready."

"Sure, Mom."

As she slipped by him, Cadeyrn asked her father about his architectural work, listening with apparent interest as he explained his most recent project for the city. In the kitchen, her mother leaned close.

"He seems very nice, Hannah."

"Oh, he is." Warmth suffused her cheeks. "He is, Mom. He's wonderful."

"He's very... polite," Karen said carefully. "Like I imagine old world aristocracy would be. And wealthy too, I assume. His clothes are perfectly tailored without that crassness of new money."

Hannah stifled a giggle. "You could say that, yes."

Karen raised her eyebrows as she looked back at the brownies, scooping vanilla ice cream over the fudge squares. "Is he really? Is that why he didn't tell us his last name?"

"I... don't know if he actually has a last name, to be honest. It's never come up."

"Is he always that polite, or is it an act for your parents?" Her mother shot her a shrewd look.

"I think he's toned it down some, actually. He'd hate to make you uncomfortable."

"Hm." Karen's tone was neutral, but Hannah saw the smile flickering over her lips. "He's very pale. Is he sick?"

"He's been... recovering from... a... *thing*. But he's much better now. He's always pale." She added, "And his hair always looks like that."

Karen chuckled softly. "It doesn't really match, you know. He's so sleek and tailored and crisp, and then this wild hair like he stuck his finger in a light socket. What kind of statement is he making?"

Hannah blinked. "I think… it's not unusual for his family. I don't think he means anything by it."

They stepped back into the dining room to hear Cadeyrn asking another question. Dave answered, smiling, then he frowned slightly. "Not to change the subject, but I have to ask. You said you'd been corresponding with Hannah for years. How did you begin this correspondence?"

"A very close friend introduced us and facilitated our long exchange of letters." Cadeyrn smiled charmingly. "I trusted his judgment. Unfortunately, I was unable to receive Hannah's letters, so she has known me much longer than I have known her. Nevertheless, she wrote to me, and I have recently had the opportunity to read all her letters to me." He glanced at her, warmth shining in his eyes. He drew the tip of one gloved finger down the condensation on the side of his glass. "She always wrote well of you. It was… intriguing… to read of such a happy family. Mine was much different."

Dave smiled, his kind face softening, then he sighed. "And I have to ask this as well. What exactly *are* your responsibilities? It's not anything illegal, is it? A matter of national security?"

Cadeyrn glanced at Hannah with an apologetic look. "Ah… no. I'm…" He sighed. "Hannah, I am not comfortable being less than forthright with your parents."

"You're right," she murmured. "I'm sorry."

Cadeyrn's answering smile made her heart flutter. "I'm a fairy," he said to her parents. "Specifically, I am the High King of Faerie, king over all Seelie peoples and lands."

Hannah couldn't help smiling at Karen and Dave's identical expressions of surprised skepticism.

Dave spoke first. "What do you mean *fairy*? Is that a euphemism for something? A political party? A club? An organized crime family?"

Cadeyrn blinked. "I had thought Faerie, and my people, were better known in the human lands, even if we are thought to be mythical."

Dave frowned. "Ah… you're saying you're a mythical creature." He glanced at Hannah. "Is this your idea of a joke?" He kept his tone light, but there was an undercurrent of worry.

"Dad, trust me." Hannah smiled reassuringly.

"Oh, I trust *you*." Dave's frown deepened as he studied Cadeyrn's face. "I'm not sure if your friend is joking or serious, and if he's serious, whether he's completely off his rocker."

Cadeyrn smiled charmingly. "Normally I'd be rather insulted by that, but fairies have kept a low profile for centuries. I'm not entirely surprised you think us fictional." He spread his gloved hands on the table, studying them for a moment. "Our world and yours are… you might say parallel, but that implies more similarities than there are. But to say that they only intersect implies that there are limited entry points, and that is also incorrect. Let us say instead that they often occupy the same space, with most of the same physical rules, but travel between them is quite restricted. Only the strongest of fairies can hope to travel between worlds. And goblins, sometimes, but their magic is of an entirely different sort, and they can't bring humans back with them." He lifted his hands and gestured gracefully. One hand flung fairy lights into the air, where they spread to float against the ceiling, shedding cool light over the room. The other produced Cara, the white owl.

Karen swallowed, her eyes widening, though she said nothing. Dave scooted his chair back a little, his eyes on the owl. "Is it real?"

"His name is Cara. He is the friend who facilitated my correspondence with your daughter." Cadeyrn murmured something to Cara, who hooted and shuffled his feet. "He is an excellent judge of character, by the way. He chose your daughter for many reasons, one of which was you." He glanced up to meet Dave's eyes. "He liked you both."

Cara swiveled his head around to look at Hannah, then hopped from Cadeyrn's hand to Hannah's shoulder. A talon caught in the fabric of her blouse. He jerked it free with an irritated hoot.

"Careful," Cadeyrn murmured. "Respect your future queen, you daft bird." With a flick of his finger, the tear in the fabric vanished as if it had never been. "My apologies. He can hold a bit of a grudge sometimes." He caught Hannah's eye. "He just likes to make his irritation known before he makes a big show of forgiving you." Cara turned to glare at Cadeyrn, then fluffed his feathers ceremoniously. He hooted softly and leaned in to nibble on Hannah's ear. "There you go," Cadeyrn's smile widened.

"What does he have to forgive Hannah for?" Karen asked.

"Oh, that's a story for another time," said Cadeyrn. "All was mended easily enough." He smiled, the light catching his sharp teeth and the feathery ends of his wild hair.

"So you're a magician?" Dave muttered. "Who keeps live owls up his sleeve?"

Karen put a hand on her husband's wrist. "Dave, it's... I don't find it as impossible to believe as you do.

Tell us a little more, then?" She turned to Cadeyrn with a slightly forced smile.

"What?" Dave looked at his wife incredulously.

"I… had an uncle." Karen shrugged. "He told me stories. Just me. He believed in magic, and fairies, and all sorts of things. He disappeared when I was young. I never thought he was quite as insane as everyone said. I'm not saying I believe it! I'm just… willing to listen."

"Harald, I believe?" Cadeyrn murmured.

Karen paled. "Um…"

"He entered our lands some years ago, yes. He's a welcome guest, though strange. Magic sometimes plays havoc on human sanity without proper training. Fairies are born magic, like centaurs and goblins, but humans are born mundane. I've given him some pointers to keep him safe; more would not be beneficial to him. He's settled near the centaurs with Comonoc's blessing."

Karen's eyes were wide. "He wasn't lying? Or crazy?"

Cadeyrn made a dismissive gesture. "Human magic, when discovered outside of Faerie, as Harald did, is nearly foreign to Faerie. It is the same force, but used in an utterly different way. I believe he is the one who devised the light-embued swords currently in use against the Shadows, although I greatly refined the technique once I was old enough to be told of the threat. That has been useful both to us and the Unseelie. He is a loyal ally to the Seelie." He shot the white owl a sharp look. "That may be one of several reasons Cara chose Hannah. Magic may run in your family. When I first began writing to her, I doubt I could have opened a way to the human world without a beacon, so to speak, on the other side. I can now, of course, but I was young."

Dave rubbed both hands over his face. "So you're not crazy?" He gazed at Cadeyrn with a faint challenge in his eyes. "You expect me to believe all this?"

The fairy king smiled thinly, then rose, the air around him crackling with restrained power. "I expect you to be wise, as I have every reason to believe you are. I love your daughter. I *wish* for your blessing upon our courtship. I wish for a family such as she wrote of, with love and kindness and generosity and warmth.

"But I am accustomed to not having my wishes granted." His eyes flashed. "I am accustomed to disappointment. I will give up my suit only when Hannah wishes me to do so. She would be an admirable queen, wise and kind and clever and good. She would also bring joy to my heart such as I have always longed for and never known. I would pour out my life to make her happy.

"I don't see what in my proposal could be unsatisfactory to a father. But then I have never been a father, so I assume you have valid reasons for your skepticism. All the same, I remind you that the decision rests with your daughter. I ask for your blessing out of courtesy and respect, not necessity." He bowed gracefully. "I thank you for the meal and the conversation."

Cadeyrn turned next to Hannah. She had the distinct feeling that he would have preferred to address her in private, but he said only, "Dearest Hannah, forgive me. My mood is clearly not the best, and I do not wish to be more discourteous than I have already been." He raised a hand to his mouth and pressed the back of his knuckles to his lips, as if forcing down unpleasant words; when he pulled his hand away, she noticed the sheen of silver blood on the dark leather of his glove. "I've never taken well to my word being doubted, and I am, perhaps, more sensitive than I should be at the moment.

Again, I ask forgiveness, and I bid you farewell." In a blink, he was gone.

The fairy lights remained, as did Cara. The white owl shuffled his feet and huffed irritably, then spread his great wings. He launched himself into the air and vanished.

SEVEN

Dave sighed heavily. "That didn't go as well as I'd hoped."

Hannah scowled. "Dad..." Then she sighed. "No, it's not all your fault. I'm sorry. It's been a rough few weeks for him."

"What exactly happened, Hannah?" her father asked. She felt the familiar rush of comfort at the sound of his voice. "Karen said you told her he was recovering from something, and then with the talk of the owl forgiving you... I want to hear the whole story." His kind brown eyes focused on her.

So she told them. The years of letters. His father's cruelty, which Cadeyrn lamented at times but never bemoaned. The war. Cadeyrn's reforms, which had made him beloved above all Faerie kings in history. Their first meeting, both sweet and awkward, the way she felt she knew him but didn't, because her imaginary Cadeyrn was so different than the real one. She blushed when she admitted her lifelong crush on her fairy pen pal, which had only strengthened after she met him.

Her visit to Faerie. How he'd ripped time apart for her, and how, when she'd turned down his proposal, he'd been hurt and then gently amused at himself, at his own hopes; how he hadn't turned frustration into bitterness. She told them of Einion and her wish, how she'd nearly cost Cadeyrn everything, and the only thing that angered him was that she'd made him a liar and endangered herself.

"Even then... even then he forgave me." She brushed tears from her eyes. "I think he's angry because he's forgotten how to hope."

Dave frowned. "I'm sorry, Hannah. I didn't mean to insult him, but... you do understand how unbelievable it sounded, don't you?"

She sighed. "I do. But if you knew him, Dad, if you saw what he did for me..."

Cara flickered into being just in front of her face, alighting on her shoulder as she squeaked in surprise. He swiveled his head to give her an enigmatic look with those bright orange eyes.

A letter sat on her lap.

Dearest Hannah,

Perhaps... perhaps I was wrong to hope so fervently. If you wish to tell me never to contact you again, I will honor that. I would understand, I suppose, though it would grieve me.

I have, in my life, very rarely been angry. Neither pain nor disappointment produce anger in me, because both are so familiar. Insult rarely produces anger.

The one thing I have always held dear, the one thing my father could not take from me, was the power of my word. For fairies, our word is broken only at the very greatest of need, and even then... even then it is not uncommon for a fairy to prefer death rather than being made a liar. I have, perhaps, held my word higher than most.

Perhaps I have been wrong. You made me reconsider that in your test with Einion; I saw the wisdom in using judgment rather than always holding my word above all. It is possible, of course, to make a vow in foolishness. Until now I have avoided such an error; I do not count my oath for your safety to be foolish at all, though it cost much.

Yet even so, even with this new wisdom that I wear uncomfortably, I found myself angry at your father for doubting me. For what reason would I lie about being a fairy? I could see no reason, and so I saw his doubt as an unbearable insult. Yet for your sake, because I love you above my pride, above my honor, above my kingdom, I pretended the insult did not sting.

I lost the ability to so dissemble when your father questioned my sanity, or questioned again whether I was lying to him. The insult, for so I felt it, stung so badly because I had hoped so very much for his respect, for his affection. Perhaps, in time, his love, as the husband of his daughter.

I was not lying when I said I would pour out my life to make you happy. I can do no other; it is all I have to give. I had hoped that even a father who doubted the existence of Faerie would see my sincerity in that.

And yet... I spoke in haste and impatience and pride. I should have been more tolerant. It is not your father's fault that knowledge of Faerie has been nearly lost to humans. I felt the sting of his doubt without understanding my own anger, without recognizing how reasonable it was for your father to doubt me. I should not have taken offense, but rather answered his objections with proof. Instead, I left you and your parents in anger because I held my pride too dear.

So I ask your forgiveness. For many years, I have tried, with every fiber of my being, to be more kind, more gentle, and more patient than my father was. To be better. To be the kind of person who is loved rather than feared. Not only to be a good king, but to be a good person... to be worthy of you.

I have failed.

I cannot ask you to be my queen if I cannot be the kind of man, the kind of king, who is worthy of your love.

My heart is wrung dry. I wish I had eloquence for you, but like all my other wishes, this one also remains unfulfilled.

Please, in your kindness, pay my respects to your parents. It was an honor to meet them.

Yours, always,

Cadeyrn

P.S. - I told your father I would not give up my suit until you wished it of me. They were brave words, spoken in a fit of pique that shames me now. Shall I break my word, or shall I continue pressing my suit when you have every reason to wish me away?

I will not write again unless you wish it. I have imposed myself upon you more than I had any right to. Nevertheless, I will always be but a wish away, should you have need of me. Fare thee well, dearest Hannah. The words probably need not be said, but I will say them anyway so you have no doubt: I love you. I always will.

WITHOUT A WORD, she handed the letter across to her parents, who read it, their heads close together.

Her father sighed, rubbing his jaw thoughtfully. "If what he's told you is true, I can't fault him for anything he's done. But I'm your father, Hannah." He looked up to meet her eyes. "Do you see how it's worrisome that he seems to have fallen in love with you after barely any interaction at all? You're lovely, of course," he smiled at her fondly, "but loveliness isn't enough. He barely knows you. Letters are more than nothing, but less than time together. An adventure and a dramatic rescue isn't enough to stake your future on."

Hannah felt her lower lip trembling and clamped her lips together, swallowing the emotion that threatened to spill over in more tears. "I know, Dad," she said. "I know it seems sudden. But it's been years for me; I've loved him since I watched cartoons on Saturday mornings!"

"I meant more for him than for you. He said he hadn't gotten your letters until just recently, didn't he?"

"Oh." She nodded reluctantly. Then she blinked. "I wish Cadeyrn would come talk to me. I have questions."

Her father's eyes widened in surprise.

CADEYRN STEPPED out of the space beside Hannah. "Yes, dearest Hannah?" His voice was nearly inaudible. His hair was as wild as ever, his eyes unnaturally bright against his marble-white skin. A short cloak hung from his shoulders, caught by a clasp with a brilliant blue gemstone that flashed the same color as his eyes.

"Thank you for coming back." Dave stood and extended his hand.

Cadeyrn hesitated, then shook his hand.

"Please, make yourself comfortable." Hannah's father gestured invitingly.

Cadeyrn's eyes flicked toward the nearest chair, then back. He tilted his head, hesitated as if he intended to say something, then sat without a word.

He's nervous, Hannah thought. Not of danger... surely he knows my family better than that. Knows his own strength. But he's afraid of what we'll say.

"Hannah said she had questions," he said, his voice soft and clear in the increasingly-awkward silence.

Dave rubbed his hands on his thighs, and Hannah realized, with some surprise, that her father was nervous too. He took a deep breath. "I've talked with Hannah, and it seems I owe you an apology. I'm sorry I didn't believe you at first. It seems I also owe you my thanks for protecting her."

Cadeyrn blinked; tightly controlled emotions flickered across his face too quickly to be interpreted. "I... thank you. All is forgiven." The taut line of his shoulders relaxed almost imperceptibly.

Hannah's father sighed, and when he spoke, Hannah knew he was deliberately softening his voice. "Please understand, I have no objection to you as a person. You seem like exactly the sort of man any father would like to call his son, or even a son-in-law. But the... surprise, I suppose, of finding out that magic is real, and that Faerie is real, is only part of my hesitation.

"It worries me that you professed such undying love so quickly. I don't want to see my daughter discarded when your infatuation runs its course. I'm sure you'd be honorable," he added hurriedly, "but I want more than that for her. I want a lifetime of love that only grows stronger, as I have with Karen." He smiled at his wife.

Cadeyrn's eyes flashed dangerously, and he opened his mouth. Dave's eyes widened as the hair on his arms stood up, static crackling in the air. Then Cadeyrn stopped, nostrils flaring as he took a controlled breath. "It seems you misunderstand me," he said softly. "This is no infatuation. My love was latent, not sudden. Do you not know that magic and love are entwined?"

At their questioning looks, his lips tightened, then his anger seemed to fade. "Your own human poets and musicians have written of this for centuries." He sighed, looking down. Hannah reached over and rested one hand on his clenched fist; he twitched, as if surprised by her touch, then gently folded his hands around hers, the smooth leather warm against her skin. "Forgive me. I assumed you knew."

He seemed to gather his thoughts before speaking again. "Infatuation is all but impossible for Fae. We have our own emotions, of course, but fleeting affection is not... natural to us. It is not part of our genetic makeup, if you will. Magic binds us... magic-users, magical creatures... to each other in myriad ways. One of those ways is love. We love as you do, with emotions and acts of self-sacrifice and generosity of spirit, but we also forge a magical connection with our intended. The connection is not entirely bounded by time. Some of the strength of the connection is derived from one or more of our possible futures, dependent on our decisions now.

"The stronger a Fae is in his control of magic, the more adept he is at perceiving the ties binding those around him. I have forged a connection with Hannah with my emotion toward her over many years, with my acts on her behalf, and with the future we may have together.

"This tie can be broken by either one of us. It is not inevitable, and our decisions are not made for us. But breaking such a tie of love, once forged, is not something that a Fae would do."

He frowned, wild eyebrows drawing downward, and took a deep breath. He spoke without looking at Hannah. "It is not... It would be like you deciding that you no longer wished to have your right hand, and deciding to chop it off. It could be done, certainly, but the decision would be unnatural.

"Hannah, being human, has no perception of this. She has the ability to decide our future." He glanced at her, his eyes guarded. "I had not yet told her this, because I wished for her to make her decision with absolute freedom. She would know, of course, that a rejection would pain me, as it would pain a human suitor. But I did not wish for her to feel undue guilt if she wished to reject my suit.

"If she were Fae, she would know all this already, and she would have some inkling of how strong the connection already is. Not as I do, because I am stronger than others and my perception is greater, but she would have confidence in the strength of the connection."

Cadeyrn swallowed, closed his eyes for a moment, and then met Dave's gaze with steady eyes. "Doubt my wisdom. Doubt my protection. Doubt the safety of a life in Faerie. Doubt my existence. But do not doubt my love for Hannah. It will not fade."

Dave looked at Hannah.

Hannah felt herself trembling, and then Cadeyrn's hands tightening around hers, reassuringly strong. "What would happen if I said no?" she whispered.

Cadeyrn stopped breathing. The thin skin on his throat moved as he swallowed. Hannah found herself transfixed by his burning eyes, the way his lips tightened before he spoke. "It is your decision, Hannah. I would accept it." He swallowed again. "It wouldn't kill me, if that's what you are asking. I... would... hope that Comonoc and Tegwen are able to conceive, because I trust none of my blood kin to rule wisely. One is promising, but he is far too young." He took an unsteady breath. "I... I... would be unable to forge a similar connection with another Fae. I gave my love to you. It cannot be transferred." His hand clenched convulsively on hers, then relaxed again. "I would rule alone. Until I died."

Those eyes bored into her, burning bright with love and desperate, fading hope.

"And you'd be fine with that?" Dave pressed, his voice almost inaudible.

"Not at all," Cadeyrn breathed. "But it is Hannah's decision, to be made without pity or guilt."

"What about love?" Hannah whispered.

"However you wish, dearest Hannah."

"I wish you'd marry me."

.

EPILOGUE

Hannah studied Cadeyrn's profile. "Were you winning the duel?"

"No."

"So… what would have happened if I hadn't wished, or if Einion hadn't granted the wish?"

Cadeyrn slanted a glance at her. "Unless I was very lucky, Einion would have killed me. Comonoc, as my designated heir, would have immediately inherited a significant amount of my power, though he would not immediately gain the skills to use it. He would, in fact, be the legitimate ruler of the Seelie. Einion, already far more powerful than Comonoc, would inherit the smaller portion of my power as the victor of the legal challenge to my rule. Einion would very likely have killed Comonoc, or… there are ways to constrain magical creatures aside from what you have seen. Comonoc might have been made captive in some way, unable to help his people as the Unseelie invaded their lands."

"Did you let him help you in the duel? He must have..." Hannah brushed sudden tears from her eyes. "He loves you, Cadeyrn, as a king and a brother. It must have hurt him so badly to see you fighting alone."

Cadeyrn tilted his head, studying her tears before reaching up to brush the pad of his thumb down her damp cheek. "Of course I did not. It was a duel. The terms are set out in the law. The crime was mine. I had to fight." He sighed, looking down at the faint sheen of her tears on his pearl-and-black skin. "Comonoc hoped to gain me a few minutes to recover my strength. It would not have been nearly enough. Einion would have killed him in moments. At least, if I fought long enough, Einion would be too weak to kill him immediately. Perhaps, with the strength of the throne in him and the combined might of the Seelie peoples, Comonoc would be able to throw off Unseelie rule in a day or two, before Einion recovered from his victory." He absently rubbed his right thumb along the place on his left arm where he had let out his blood into the goblet. The silver-scabbed line was gone as if it had never been, his pearly skin marked only by the charcoal-black scars of war magic. "I cannot say I believed this would happen, but it was a faint hope. I fought for it, because I had nothing left to fight for." He licked his lips, then looked up to meet Hannah's gaze. "You were safe. I may have failed as a king to protect my people, but I did not fail you."

The words twisted in her heart. She could not breathe. She buried her face in her hands.

Cadeyrn made a tiny, startled sound. "Hannah! What is wrong?"

"No wonder you hated me," she whispered. "I didn't understand how you could be so angry when I just wanted to help you. But now I know."

Cadeyrn bent over her hands, clasping them between his, kissing them again and again. His spidersilk hair brushed her face, and she smelled frost and ozone, pine and cinnamon and magic. He spoke with his lips against her knuckles, interspersing the words with kisses. "Forgive me, Hannah. I did not mean to hurt you." He sighed, resting his head against their twined fingers before straightening. "What you did may have been done in ignorance of fairy law, innocent of the repercussions, but it was brave and kind and good. It was wrong of me to fault you for that. I am not... accustomed... to anyone thinking more of me than of their own safety. That is no excuse, but it is the truth. I did not fully appreciate how magnificent you are." His eyes warmed when he saw her cheeks flush. "I was so angry because I was so terrified. The simplest thing for Einion to do would have been to give you a sword and let you 'help' me in the duel. He would claim he'd granted your wish, you'd be dead, and I was far too weak to turn back time again, even for you. I would have killed myself trying, but I would have failed."

Hannah closed her eyes, trying not to imagine it. *Cadeyrn white as marble, swaying, silver blood on his lips and coming from his nose. Einion's mocking smile, sharp teeth flashing in the cold light. The wind whipping her clothes as Einion pulled the sword from her belly, blood drips like rubies on the edge.* She couldn't exactly imagine the pain, but she imagined the terror and despair. *The world turning inside out, juttering sideways, shards of reality recombining into the present. Pain. Blood on her hands, trying to keep her entrails where they belonged. Time shattering, bits and pieces flying apart, a disorienting roar that came from everywhere and no-*

where. Cara's talons digging into her shoulders, pulling her back through time and space. The world collapsing into itself. Cadeyrn falling to his knees, still staring at her. Silver blood. Red blood. Silver blood.

"Hannah," Cadeyrn's voice snapped her back to reality. "Don't think about it." His blue eyes flashed, his strange eyebrows drawn down in a frown. "And I could *never* hate you."

Hannah said, "Why…" Her voice shook, and she sniffed and cleared her throat. "Why didn't he do that, then?"

Cadeyrn sighed, and she glanced at him.

He's still more tired than he'd like me to think.

"He's Unseelie." He absently rubbed his thumb over her knuckles as he thought. "Fairies… Unseelie believe they are just as natural as Seelie. We Seelie, at least some of us, believe Unseelie were twisted in the distant past. They are contradictions, at least as we understand them. They delight in keeping their word, but they also delight in deceit. They revere Einion, who is widely understood to be a good king in the Unseelie way, but they also attempt coups at every opportunity. Yet when the opportunity came to truly have him deposed, they were grieved by it. They are chaos, but they delight in games and winning by the rules, however complex and convoluted and contradictory those rules may be.

"Einion probably had no intent to cheat you, as you understood it and accused him. The law stood on your side. Unseelie more often run afoul of the law than Seelie do, because they more often misunderstand the concept of 'cheating.' I don't fully understand his intent, but I can guess.

"If he had simply handed you a sword and then killed you, he would have lost the fun of defeating a challenging opponent. He would have enjoyed my despair, but the lure was not enough. He may also have feared that would be too close to cheating and feared the penalty. Besides, he wanted a more subtle victory.

"His challenge was clever. In accepting the challenge, you accepted that my life and my kingdom were the stakes. He—"

"If I hadn't accused him of cheating me..." Hannah stared at him with horrified eyes. "Would he have killed you? I thought..."

Cadeyrn tilted his head to the side, considering. "Perhaps. But his offer to you at the end was genuine. He *was* impressed. He wanted you to consent to stay with him."

Hannah felt her heart thudding raggedly. "For how long?" she whispered.

"As long as possible." His lips tightened. "He might have kept me alive as an incentive, so to speak. My life and kingdom were forfeit already, but if he offered a temporary reprieve... He thought it was worth the attempt. More importantly, he delighted in using you to defeat me. He knew I loved you; using you as the means of my defeat would satisfy every Unseelie bone in his body."

Silver blood. Red blood. Silver blood. She shuddered.

He kissed her fingers again, his lips hot against her skin. "Hannah, do not think about it. It did not happen." He brushed her hair back from her face, his fingertips grazing her temple and lingering at her ear, trailing feather-light down her neck before he pulled away. "You're imagining possibilities. But possibilities are not facts." He smiled, showing his sharp teeth. "And even facts can sometimes be changed."

Hannah closed her eyes, breathing in magic and power and electric desire. "Will you kiss me, Cadeyrn?"

His lips found hers, and the rest of her questions were lost in the dissolution of time and space. Frost and pine and magic and heat and desire and tenderness rippled through her, stealing her breath, leaving her gasping, dizzy, laughing, comforted.

Cadeyrn trailed kisses over her cheek, down her neck, up to her ear. "Whenever you wish, my dearest Hannah."

C. J. BRIGHTLEY

C. J. Brightley lives in Northern Virginia with her husband and young daughter. She holds degrees from Clemson University and Texas A&M. She welcomes visitors and messages at her website, www.cjbrightley.com.

THINGS UNSEEN

A LONG-FORGOTTEN SONG
BOOK 1

CHAPTER 1

Researching this thesis is an exercise in dedication, frustration, making up stuff, pretending I know what I'm doing, and wondering why nothing adds up. Aria swirled her coffee and stared at the blank page in her notebook.

Why did I decide to study history? She flipped back to look at her notes and sighed. She couldn't find enough information to even form a coherent thesis. The records were either gone, or had never existed in the first place. *Something* had happened when the Revolution came to power, but she didn't know what, and she couldn't even pinpoint exactly when.

The nebulous idea she'd had for her research seemed even more useless now. She'd been trying to find records of how things had changed since the Revolution, how the city had grown and developed. There were official statistics on the greater prosperity, the academic success of the city schools, and the vast reduction in crime. The statistics didn't mention the abandoned buildings, the missing persons, or any grumbling against the curfew. At least it was later now; for a year, curfew had been at dusk.

She glanced around the bookstore at the other patrons. A man wearing a business suit was browsing in the self-help section, probably trying to improve his public speaking. A girl, probably another student judging by her worn jeans and backpack, was sitting on the floor in the literary fiction section, completely engrossed in a book.

Aria flipped to the front of the book again. It was a memoir of someone she'd never heard of. She'd picked it up almost at random, and flipped to the middle, hoping to find something more interesting than dead ends. The words told of a walk in the forest, and for a moment Aria was there, her nose filled with the scents of pine and loam, her eyes dazzled by the sunlight streaming through the leaves swaying above her. She blinked, and the words were there but the feeling was gone. Rereading the passage, she couldn't figure out why she'd been caught up with such breathless realism.

It wasn't that the words were so profound; she was confident they were not. Something had caught her though, and she closed her eyes to imagine the forest again, as if it were a memory. Distant, faded, perhaps not even her memory. A memory of something she'd seen in a movie, perhaps, or a memory of a dream she'd had as a child.

Something about it troubled her, and she meant to come back to it. Tonight, though, she had other homework, and she pushed the book aside.

Dandra's Books was an unassuming name for the best bookstore in all of the North Quadrant. Dandra was a petite, grey-haired lady with a warm smile. She also had the best map collection, everything from ancient history, both originals and reproductions, to modern maps of cities both near and far, topographical maps, water currents, and everything else. She carried the new releases and electronic holdings that were most in demand, but what made the store unique was the extensive and ever-changing selection of used and antique books. If it could be found, Dandra could find it. Aria suspected she maintained an unassuming storefront because she didn't want demand to increase; business was sufficient to pay the bills and she refused to hire help.

Dandra also made tolerable coffee, an important consideration for a graduate student. Aria had spent hours studying there as an undergraduate; it had the same air of productive intellectualism as the university library, but without the distraction of other groups of students having more fun than she was. She'd found it on a long, meandering walk avoiding some homework. Something about the place made concentrating easier.

Except when it came to her thesis. Aria told herself that she was investigating what resources were available before she narrowed her focus. But sometimes, when she stared at the blank pages, she almost admitted to herself the truth, that she was frustrated with her professors, her thesis, and the Empire itself. She didn't have a good explanation, and she hadn't told anyone.

Something about this image of the forest felt true in a way that nothing had felt for a very long time. It was evidence. Evidence of *what*, she wasn't sure. But definitely evidence.

She finished her homework and packed her bag. She put a bookmark in the memoir and reshelved it, resolving that she would come back later and read it a bit more. It was already late, and she had an early class the next day.

After class there were errands, and homework, and more class, and lunch with a boy who'd seemed almost likable until he talked too much about his dysfunctional family and his abiding love for his ex-girlfriend, who lived down the hall in his apartment building. It was a week before she made it back to Dandra's.

The book was gone.

Dandra shook her head when Aria asked about it. "I don't know what book you mean. I've never had a book like that."

Aria stared at her in disbelief. "You saw me read it last week. It was called *Memories Kept* or something like that. *Memory Keeper*, maybe. Don't you remember? I was sitting there." She pointed.

Dandra gave her a sympathetic look. "You've been studying too much, Aria. I'm sorry. I don't have that book. I don't think I ever did."

Aria huffed in frustration and bought a cup of coffee. She put too much sugar and cream in it and sat by the window at the front. She stared at the people as they came in, wondering if her anger would burn a hole in the back of someone's coat. It didn't, but the mental picture amused her.

Not much else did. The thesis was going nowhere, and the only thing that kept her interest was a line of questions that had no answers and a book that didn't exist.

Was the degree worth anything anyway? She'd studied history because she enjoyed stories, wanted to learn about the past. But the classes had consisted almost entirely of monologues by the professors about the strength of the Empire and how much better things were now after the Revolution. Her papers had alternated between parroting the professors' words, and uneasy forays into the old times. The research was hard, and getting harder.

The paper she'd written on the Revolution, on how John Sanderhill had united the warring factions, had earned an F. Dr. Corten had written "Your implication that Sanderhill ordered the assassination of Gerard Neeson is patently false and betrays an utter lack of understanding of the morality of the Revolution. I am unable to grade this paper higher than an F, in light of such suspect scholarship and patriotism." Yet Aria had cited her source clearly and had been careful not to take a side on the issue, choosing merely to note that it was one possible explanation for Neeson's disappearance at the height of the conflict. Not even the most likely.

For a history department, her professors were remarkably uninterested in exploring the past. She scowled at her coffee as it got colder. What was the point of history, if you couldn't learn from it? The people in history weren't perfect, any more than people now were. But surely, as scholars, they should be able to admit that imperfect people and imperfect decisions could yield lessons and wisdom.

It wasn't as if it was ancient history either. The Revolution had begun less than fifteen years ago. One would think information would be available. Memories should be clear.

But they weren't.

The man entered Dandra's near dusk. He wore no jacket against the winter cold, only a threadbare short-sleeved black shirt. His trousers were dark and equally worn, the cuffs skimming bare ankles. His feet were bare too, and that caught her attention.

He spoke in a low voice, but she was curious, so she listened hard and heard most of what he said. "I need the maps, Dandra."

"You know I don't have those."

"I'll pay."

"I don't have them." Dandra took a step back as he leaned forward with his hands resting on the desk. "I told you before, I can't get them. I still can't."

"I was told you could on good authority." His voice stayed very quiet, but even Aria could hear the cold anger. "Should I tell Petro he was wrong about you?"

"Are you threatening me?" Dandra's eyes widened, but Aria couldn't tell if it was in fear or in anger.

"I'm asking if Petro was wrong."

"Tell Petro I did my best. I couldn't get them." Dandra clasped her hands together and drew back, her shoulders against the wall, and Aria realized she was terrified. Of the man in the black shirt, or of Petro, or possibly both.

Aria rose. "Excuse me? Can I help you find something?" She smiled brightly at him.

He stared at Dandra for a long moment, then turned away. He brushed past Aria and out the door without looking at her, and disappeared into the darkness.

Dandra looked at her with wide eyes. "That wasn't wise, but thank you."

"Who is he?"

Dandra shook her head. "Don't ask questions you don't want to know the answer to. Go home, child. It's late."

Made in the USA
Columbia, SC
03 October 2017